The Metamorphosis

FRANZ KAFKA

PRESTWICK HOUSE
LITERARY TOUCHSTONE CLASSICS™
P.O. BOX 658 • CLAYTON, DELAWARE 19938

EDITOR: Paul Moliken

TRANSLATOR: M. A. Roberts

DESIGN: Larry Knox

PRODUCTION: Jerry Clark

PRESTWICK HOUSE
LITERARY TOUCHSTONE CLASSICS™
P.O. BOX 658 • CLAYTON, DELAWARE 19938
TEL: 1.800.932.4593
FAX: 1.888.718.9333
WEB: www.prestwickhouse.com

Prestwick House Teaching Units™, Activity Packs™, and Response Journals™ are the perfect complement for these editions. To purchase teaching resources for this book, visit www.prestwickhouse.com/material

ISBN   978-1-58049-581-3

The Metamorphosis

BY FRANZ KAFKA

CONTENTS

NOTES

What is a literary classic and why are these classic works important to the world?

A literary classic is a work of the highest excellence that has something important to say about life and/or the human condition and says it with great artistry. A classic, through its enduring presence, has withstood the test of time and is not bound by time, place, or customs. It speaks to us today as forcefully as it spoke to people one hundred or more years ago and as forcefully as it will speak to people of future generations. For this reason, a classic is said to have universality.

This new translation of *The Metamorphosis* relies on the original German text, published in 1915 by Kurt Wolff. We felt that a new translation was necessary because various English versions we examined seemed to take liberties with the text, were too simply written, or lacked Kafka's offbeat humor, most of which actually does translate well.

Additionally, many of Kafka's sentences tend to be quite long, with convoluted syntax and punctuation. To remain faithful to the German text, this Prestwick House translation makes every effort to follow Kafka's actual style and word choice as closely as possible, while still creating an artful English rendition.

We also include a list of difficult vocabulary words and a set of glossary notes that highlight literary devices and that explore some of the possible shades of meaning which are present in the original German.

If you have any comments about this book, whether positive or negative, feel free to contact us. We hope that you will enjoy this new translation and find it an accurate representation of one of the twentieth century's masterpieces.

M. A. Roberts

Franz Kafka was born to a Jewish family in Prague in 1883. He lived with his family most of his life and believed his father to be unfeeling and domineering. After his two older brothers died, he became the eldest of four children. He had three younger sisters. Kafka obtained a law degree and wrote in his spare time while working for an agency affiliated with the government. His works frequently portray stifling, bureaucratic institutions and oppressive father figures. Although he was engaged twice, he never married; his relationships with women tended to be difficult and troubled. Kafka died in 1924 of the tuberculosis from which he suffered since contracting it seven years earlier.

The Metamorphosis was first published in 1915. Kafka's friend Max Brod undertook the job of editing and distributing Kafka's works after his death, defying Kafka's wish that all of his writings be burned. His stories are deeply steeped in existentialism and are rife with symbolism. Because there are many elements in his stories that appear irrational or surreal, the adjective *Kafkaesque* has come to indicate that a situation is absurd or that a character is alienated from others.

READING POINTERS

Reading Pointers for Sharper Insights

To better appreciate Kafka's *Metamorphosis*, it is essential to understand some of the existentialist ideas and beliefs that influenced his thoughts and writings.

Existentialism, a philosophy that became popular during the 19th century, generally asserts that destiny is chosen (rather than predetermined or ordained), that individuals must decide for themselves what they will believe is true, and that the greatest truths (such as the existence of God or the morality of any one act) cannot be rationally determined. Self-sufficiency or independence from other people is another ideal that existentialism extols. This philosophy also generally values the primacy of momentary existence: The only morality is that which is useful at the present time.

Overall, existentialism admits that stark individualism and self-determination will lead to personal anxiety (or *angst*). Complete and total freedom of choice can overwhelm a person who is unhindered by any consideration for the past, for other people, or for the good of society as a whole. This can often lead to the kind of isolation and despair that Gregor experiences in *The Metamorphosis*. Gregor is a type of anti-hero who faces a choice about whether or not to continue upholding the existentialist ideal.

The Metamorphosis is a highly symbolic text; many events, objects, and people represent or illustrate certain other, more complicated, ideas. The plot itself does not make rational sense; it depends entirely on the reader's acceptance of Gregor's transformation. Note that Kafka never answers or even addresses the major question implicit in the novel: How and why did Gregor become a bug?

As you read *The Metamorphosis*, note the following recurrent themes:

1. The following existentialist ideas can be found in the text:
    - The universe is indifferent and often apparently hostile to humans.
    - Human existence is unexplainable. /purposeless /meaningless
    - Isolation, anxiety, and despair are part of life.
    - People judge life according to individual experiences.
    - Freedom of choice exists, but so do the consequences of one's actions.
    - A person's own convictions, not external rules, determine truth.

2. Gregor's transformation and new physical form may seem to be the most significant plot details, but they are merely the catalysts for story development and ways for Kafka to express his ideas. Gregor's relationship with the family, the choices he makes or doesn't make, and the various symbols in the book are more important elements.

3. Kafka explains, at various places in the book, that in a time period before the novel starts, Gregor once provided for the needs of his entire family. Note how the family comes to view Gregor's lack of ability to earn money over the course of the story.

4. Gregor is not the only character who undergoes a metamorphosis during the course of the story. The rest of the family, especially his sister, also experiences a transformation. Note how the family members change and how their attitudes or actions toward Gregor also change.

5. Kafka is often celebrated as an especially effective critic of totalitarianism and its faceless bureaucracy. What can you find in *The Metamorphosis* that supports this opinion?

6. Note how Gregor thinks about and deals with his situation, how he relates to his family, what he thinks about his job, and what his responses to change are. Are these responses what one would expect in such a dramatic and catastrophic transformation?

7. Gregor's room can be interpreted as symbolizing himself; the rest of the house and the city may be representative of the rest of society. Changes in the room and changes in Gregor's ability to enter or perceive the world outside of his room indicate his degree of isolation from other people.

8. Note the recurrence of the number three throughout the novel: three tenants, three other members of the family, three doors into Gregor's room, and so on. This may be a religious reference or theme that Kafka is creating.

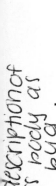

C H A P T E R   I

THE METAMORPHOSIS[1]

AS GREGOR SAMSA awoke one morning out of restless dreams, he found himself in bed, transformed into a gargantuan pest.[2] He lay on his hard, armored back and saw, as he raised his head a little, his domed, brown belly, divided into arched segments; he could hardly keep the bed sheets from sliding from his stomach's height completely to the floor. His numerous legs, lamentably thin in comparison to his new girth, flickered helplessly before his eyes.[3]

"What has happened to me?" he thought. It was no dream. His room, a proper room for a human being (albeit a little too small), lay still between the four familiar walls. Above the table, upon which a collection of sample cloth goods was spread out in stacks—Samsa was a traveling salesman—hung the picture which he had cut out of an illustrated magazine a little while ago and set in a pretty gilt frame. It depicted a woman who, with a fur hat and a fur boa, sat erect, lifting up in the direction of the viewer a solid fur muff into which her entire forearm had disappeared.[4]

Gregor's glance then turned to the window, and the dreary weather—one heard raindrops falling upon the window ledge—made him quite melancholy. "How would it be if

description of his body as a bug

animal like features

[1]*Kafka's title actually translates as The Transformation. See glossary note on Metamorphosis.*

[2]Pest *could also be* vermin. *See glossary.*

[3]*The description of Gregor's body as rounded may allude to the idea that Gregor, once a man, is now less of a man, a non-male, or an asexual creature.*

[4]*The picture may allude to some sort of sexual confusion as one of Gregor's problems. Note that the lady's fur covering makes her appear almost like an animal. See glossary note on Mother, Sister.*

I kept sleeping for a little while longer and forgot all this foolishness," he thought; but this was entirely impractical, for he was accustomed to sleeping on his right side, and in his present circumstances, he couldn't bring himself into this position. No matter how hard he threw himself onto his right side, he always rolled again into a prone position. He tried it a full hundred times, closing his eyes because he had to avoid seeing the wriggling legs, and gave up trying when he began to feel a slight, dull pain in his side that he had hitherto not felt.

"Oh God," he thought, "what a strenuous occupation I've chosen![5] Always on the road, day out, day in. The rigors of the job are much greater than if I were working locally, and, furthermore, the nuisances of traveling are always imposed upon me—the worries about train connections, bad meals at irregular intervals, fleeting human contact that is ever-changing, never lasting, and never expected to be genuine. To the devil with it all!" He felt a slight itching on the top of his abdomen. He slowly pushed himself on his back closer to the bedpost so that he could lift his head more easily, found the itchy area, which was entirely covered with small white spots—he did not know what to make of them—and wanted to feel the place with a leg. But he retracted it immediately, for the contact felt like a cold shower all over him.

He slid back again into his earlier position. "This getting up early," he thought, "makes one completely idiotic. A man must have his sleep. Other travelers live like harem women.[6] For instance, when I come back to the inn during the course of the morning to write up the necessary orders, these gentlemen are just sitting down to breakfast. If I were to try that with my boss, I'd be thrown out on the spot.

"Who knows, though—that might not be such a bad thing. If I didn't hold back for my parents' sake, I'd have quit ages ago. I would go to the boss and state my opinion out loud from the bottom of my heart. He would've fallen right off his desk! He's a strange sort, sitting up on that desk and speaking down to the employee from on high like that. Moreover, the boss has trouble hearing, and one has to step up close to him. At any rate, hope is not completely gone: once I've collected

[5] *Gregor's first thoughts upon waking up as a creature are not related to his physical form, but the state of affairs in his life. He is focusing almost entirely on how much he despises his work.*

[6] *This statement about harem women is an ironic one. See glossary note on Harem Women.*

trying to figure things out; doesn't understand

existentialism – choose your own

what is he gonna do w/ his job? scared

the money to pay off my parents' debt to him—that should take another five or six years—I'll do it for sure. I'll cut all ties and move on. In any case, right now I have to get up; my train leaves at five."

He saw the alarm clock over there, ticking on the chest of drawers. "Good God!" he thought. It was half past six, and the hands were going quietly on. It was past the half hour, almost quarter to seven. Shouldn't the alarm have sounded? One could see from the bed that it had been properly set for four o'clock. Certainly it had rung. And was it even possible for one to sleep quietly through the noise that made even the furniture shake?[7] Now, he certainly hadn't had a peaceful sleep, but apparently it was deep nonetheless. But what should he do now? The next train left at seven o'clock. To catch that one, he would have to make a mad dash; his assortment of wares wasn't packed up yet, and he really didn't feel particularly fresh and active. And even if he caught the train, there was no way to avoid those storm clouds brewing over the boss' head, because the firm's errand boy would've waited for the five o'clock train and reported the news of his absence long ago. He was the boss's minion, without backbone or intelligence.[8] Well then, what if he called in sick? But that would be extremely embarrassing and suspicious, because during his five years' service Gregor hadn't been sick even once. The boss would certainly come with the doctor from the health insurance company and would reproach his parents for their lazy son, cutting short all objections with the comments from the insurance doctor, who thought everyone was completely healthy but work-shy. And besides, would the doctor in this case be totally wrong?[9] Apart from an excessive drowsiness after the long sleep, Gregor, in fact, felt quite well and even had an especially strong appetite. As he was thinking all this over in the greatest haste, without being able to make the decision to get out of bed (the clock struck quarter to seven), there was a cautious knock on the door near the head of the bed. "Gregor," a voice called—it was mother. "It's quarter to seven. Don't you want to be on your way?" The soft voice! Gregor was startled when he heard his voice answering. It was clearly and unmistakably his earlier voice, but in

(margin annotation: ironic)

[7] *Kafka uses the pronoun* one *to refer to people in general. See glossary note on* One.

[8] *The irony of this comment is obvious: Gregor is as much a* minion *of the boss as the errand boy is. See glossary note on* Backbone.

[9] *Gregor is conceding that his condition is as much mental as it is physical.*

it was intermingled, as if from below, an irrepressibly painful squeaking, which left the words positively distinct only in the first moment and distorted them in the next moment, so that one didn't know if one had heard correctly. Gregor wanted to answer in detail and explain everything, but in these circumstances he confined himself to saying, "Yes, yes, thank you mother. I'm getting up right away." Because of the wooden door, the change in Gregor's voice was not really noticeable outside, so his mother calmed down with this explanation and shuffled off. However, as a result of the short conversation, the other family members became aware that Gregor was unexpectedly still at home, and already his father was knocking on one side door, weakly but with his fist. "Gregor, Gregor," he called out. "What's going on?" And, after a short while, he urged him on again in a deeper voice: "Gregor! Gregor!" At the other side door, however, his sister knocked lightly. "Gregor? Are you not well? Do you need anything?" Gregor directed answers at both sides: "I'm almost done." He made an effort with the most careful articulation and by inserting long pauses between the individual words to remove everything remarkable from his voice. Father turned back to his breakfast. However, the sister whispered, "Gregor, open the door—I beg you." Gregor had no intention of opening the door, but congratulated himself on his precaution, acquired from traveling, of locking all doors during the night, even at home.

First, he wanted to get out of bed quietly and without disturbance, get dressed, above all to have breakfast, and only then consider further action, for—he noticed this clearly—by thinking things over in bed he would not reach any sensible conclusions. He already remembered that he had often felt a light pain in bed, perhaps the result of some awkward sleeping position, which later turned out to be purely imaginary when he stood up, and he was eager to see how his present fantasies would gradually fade away. That the change in his voice was nothing other than the onset of a real chill, an occupational illness of commercial travelers—of that he had not the slightest doubt.[10]

It was very easy to throw aside the blanket; he needed only to push himself up a little, and it fell by itself. But to continue

[10]*This is, perhaps, the closest that Gregor ever comes to examining his own situation. He is convinced that his condition is an illusion or a temporary illness.*

The Metamorphosis 17

was difficult, particularly because he was so unusually wide. He needed arms and hands to push himself upright. In the place of these, however, he had only a lot of little legs, which were incessant in their various motions and which, moreover, he was unable to control. If he wanted to bend one of them, then it was the first to stretch itself out, and meanwhile, if he finally succeeded in doing what he wanted with this limb, all the others, as if left free, moved around in an excessively painful agitation. "But I must not stay in bed uselessly," said Gregor to himself.

At first he wanted to get out of bed with the lower part of his body, but this lower part—which, by the way, he had not yet looked at and which he also couldn't clearly imagine—proved itself too difficult to move. The attempt went so slowly. When, having become almost frantic, he finally hurled himself forward with all his force and without thinking, he chose his direction incorrectly, and he hit the lower bedpost hard. The burning pain he felt taught him that the lower part of his body was, at the moment, perhaps the most sensitive.

Thus, he tried to get his upper body out of the bed first and turned his head carefully toward the edge of the bed. He managed to do this easily, and in spite of its width and weight, his body mass at last slowly followed the turning of his head. But as he finally raised his head outside the bed in the open air, he became anxious about moving forward any further in this manner, for if he allowed himself eventually to fall by this process, it would take a miracle to prevent his head from getting injured. And, at all costs, he must not lose consciousness right now; he would prefer to remain in bed.

However, after a similar effort whereby he brought himself with a deep sigh back into his prone position and once again saw his little legs fighting one another with even more fury than before, if such a thing were possible, and didn't see any chance of bringing peace and order to this arbitrary movement, he told himself again that he couldn't possibly remain in bed and that it might be the most reasonable thing to sacrifice everything if there were even the slightest hope of freeing himself from bed in the process. At the same moment, however, he didn't forget now and then to remember that the calm and calmest contemplation would be much better than desperate conclusions. At such moments, he directed his gaze as precisely as he could toward the window, but unfortunately there was little confidence or encouragement to be had from a glance at the morning mist, which concealed even the other side of the narrow street. "Already seven o'clock," he told himself at the latest striking of the alarm clock, "already seven o'clock and still such a fog." And, for a little while longer, he lay quietly, breathing weakly, as if waiting, perhaps, for his real and natural proportions to return out of the complete stillness.[11]

constantly frustrated b/c of reality + forces turning against him

[11]*Gregor's decision in favor of inaction is an indication of how well he fits the existentialist ideal. See glossary note on Gregor's Decision.*

accepting his position; determining who + what you are

But then he said to himself: "Prior to it striking quarter past seven, I must by all means abandon this bed completely. Besides, by then, someone from the office will arrive to inquire about me, because the office will open before seven o'clock." And he made an effort then to rock the entire length of his body out of the bed with a uniform motion. If he let himself fall out of the bed in this way, his head, which in the course of the fall he intended to lift up sharply, would in all likelihood remain uninjured. His back seemed to be hard; nothing would really happen to that as a result of the fall on the carpet. His greatest reservation was a worry about the loud crash that the fall must cause and which presumably would cause fright, or at the very least concern, on the other side of the doors. It had to be risked, though.

When Gregor was already sticking out halfway off the bed—the new method was more of a game than a strain since he needed only to rock consistently with a jerking motion—it struck him how easy all this would be if someone were to come to his aid.[12] Two strong people—he thought of his father and the maid—would have been entirely sufficient. They would only have had to slide their arms under his dome-like back in order to pry him out of bed, to bend down with their load, and then merely to exercise patience and care so that he completely swung over onto the floor, where hopefully his little legs would acquire some sense. Now, quite apart from the fact that the doors were locked, should he really call out for help? In spite of all his distress, he was unable to suppress a smile at this idea.

[12]*Gregor's idea of desiring others' help is his first step toward complete reliance on his family.*

Because he was rocking so strongly, he was already at the point where he could hardly maintain his balance, and very soon he would have to definitively choose, for in five minutes it would be quarter past seven—and there was a ring at the door of the apartment. "That's someone from the office," he told himself, and he was almost paralyzed because his small legs only danced around all the faster. For one moment, everything remained still. "They aren't opening it," Gregor said to himself, biased in favor of this idea by some absurd hope. But, naturally, the maid's firm steps went as they always did and opened the door. Gregor needed to hear only the first word of the visitor's greeting to recognize immediately who it was—the firm's attorney himself. Why was Gregor the only one condemned to work in a firm where, at the slightest lapse, someone immediately attracted the greatest suspicion? Were all the employees then collectively, one and all, scoundrels; was there among them then not one truly devoted person who, failing to take advantage of the morning hours for work, would go mad because of pangs of conscience and would, therefore, not be fit to leave bed? Was it truly insufficient to have an apprentice inquire—if such interrogation were even necessary; did the attorney need to come himself, and through his coming, did the entire innocent family need to be shown that the investigation of this suspicious affair could be entrusted only to the attorney's understanding? And, more as a consequence of the excited state in which this idea put Gregor than as a result of an actual decision, he swung himself with all his might out of the bed. There was a loud thud, but it was not really a crash. The fall was absorbed somewhat by the carpet and, in addition, his back was more elastic than Gregor had thought,[13] and for this reason the dull noise was not conspicuous at all. But he had not held his head up with sufficient care and had hit it; because of the pain and irritation, he turned his head and rubbed it on the carpet.

"Something has fallen in there," said the attorney in the next room on the left. Gregor tried to imagine to himself whether anything similar to what was happening to him today could have also happened at some point to the attorney; at the very least, one had to concede the possibility of

[13]*Another reference to Gregor's lack of backbone. See glossary.*

[14]*Is Gregor imply-*
ing that the
attorney was once
transformed into
a bug, and, by
extension, that
all humans are
insects?

such a thing.[14] However, as if to give a rough answer to this question, the attorney now, allowing his polished shoes to creak, took a few determined steps in the next room. From the neighboring room on the right the sister was whispering to inform Gregor: "Gregor, the attorney is here." "I know," said Gregor to himself; but he did not dare raise his voice loud enough so that his sister could hear.

"Gregor," his father now said from the neighboring room on the left, "the head attorney has come and is asking why you did not leave on the early train. We don't know what we should tell him. Besides, he also wants to speak to you person-ally. So please open the door. He will certainly be good enough to forgive the mess in your room."

In the middle of all this, the attorney called out in a friendly way, "Good morning, Mr. Samsa." "He is not well," said his mother to the attorney, while his father was still talk-ing at the door. "He is not well, sir, believe me, good attorney. Otherwise, how would Gregor miss a train! The boy has noth-ing in his head except business. I'm almost angry that he never goes out at night; right now he's been in the city eight days, but he's been at home every evening. He sits here with us at the table and quietly reads the newspaper or studies his travel

[15]*A small saw used*
to cut intricate
woodwork. See
glossary note on
Fretsaw.

schedules. Doing fretsaw[15] work is also quite a diversion for him. For instance, he cut out a small frame over the course of two or three evenings; you'd be amazed how pretty it is—it's hanging right inside the room—you'll see it immediately, as soon as Gregor opens the door. Anyway, I'm happy that you're here, good attorney; by ourselves, we wouldn't have brought Gregor to the point of opening the door; he's so stub-born, and he's certainly not well, although he denied that this morning."

"I'm coming right away," said Gregor slowly and deliber-ately; he didn't move, so as not to lose one word of the con-versation. "My dear lady, I cannot explain it to myself in any other way," said the attorney. "I hope it is nothing serious. On the other hand, I must also say that we business people—for better or worse, however one looks at it—very often simply have to overcome a minor infirmity for business concerns." "So can the good attorney come in to see you now?" asked the impatient father as he knocked once again on the door. "No," said Gregor. In the adjacent room on the left, an embarrassing stillness set in; in the adjacent room on the right, the sister began to sob.

Why didn't the sister go to the others? She'd probably just gotten up out of bed and hadn't even started to get dressed yet. Then why was she crying? Because he wasn't getting up and wasn't letting the attorney in, because he was in danger of losing his position, and because then his boss would badger his parents once again with the old demands? At this point, those worries were completely unnecessary. Gregor was still here and wasn't thinking at all about deserting his family. At the moment, he was lying right there on the carpet, and no one who knew about his condition would've seriously requested that he let the attorney in. But because of this minor rudeness, for which he would easily find a suitable excuse later, Gregor could not be immediately dismissed. It seemed to Gregor that it might be far more reasonable to leave him in peace at the moment instead of disturbing him with crying and persuasion. But it was that very uncertainty that distressed the others and excused their behavior.

"Mr. Samsa," called out the attorney with a raised voice, "what's the matter? You are barricading yourself in your room, answering with a mere yes or no, making serious and unnecessary troubles for your parents, and neglecting (I mention this only incidentally) your commercial duties in a truly unheard-of manner. I am speaking here in the name of your parents and your supervisors, and I am asking you earnestly for an immediate, clear explanation. I am amazed; I am amazed. I thought I knew you as a calm, reasonable person, and now you appear suddenly to want to start parading about with peculiar moods. The supervisor mentioned to me earlier this very day a possible explanation for your neglect—it concerned the collection of cash entrusted to you a short while ago—but, in truth, I gave him my word of honor that this explanation could not be correct.[16] However, now I see here your unfathomable stubbornness, and I am completely losing any desire to stick out my neck for you at all. And your position is certainly not the most secure one. I originally had

[16]*The attorney mentions his suspicion that Gregor may have stolen some money from work. Although this is neither confirmed nor disproved, it is a curious note on what might have happened before the story began.*

[17] *Besides the pos-
sible theft of cash,
it also seems
that Gregor has
been lazy, since,
according to the
attorney, he hasn't
made any sales at
all lately.*

the intention of keeping all of this between the two of us,
but since you are letting me waste my time here uselessly, I
don't know why your parents shouldn't also learn about it.
Your performance has also been quite unsatisfactory of late;
it's hardly the time of year for making exceptional sales, we
acknowledge that, but there is no such thing at all as a time
of year for making no sales, Mr. Samsa; such a thing will not
be permitted."[17]

"But attorney, sir," called Gregor, beside himself and, in his
agitation, forgetting everything else, "I'm opening the door
immediately, this very moment. A slight indisposition, a dizzy
spell, has prevented me from getting up. I'm still lying in bed
right now. But I'm already quite refreshed again. I'm climb-
ing out of bed this instant. Just a short moment of patience!
Things are not going as well as I thought. But I'm still well.
How suddenly this can overcome a person! Only yesterday
evening everything was fine with me, my parents certainly
know that; actually just yesterday evening, I had a slight
premonition. People must have seen that in me. Indeed, why
didn't I report that to the office! But people always think that
they'll get over sickness without having to stay at home. My
dear sir, attorney! Spare my parents! There is really no basis
for the accusations which you are now leveling against me,
and until now, nobody has mentioned a word of this to me.
Perhaps you have not read the latest orders which I shipped.
Moreover, now I'm setting out on my trip on the eight o'clock
train; the few hours of rest have strengthened me. Attorney,
sir, don't tarry; I will be at the office in person right away;
please have the kindness to say that and to give my regards to
the supervisor!"

While Gregor was quickly blurting all this out, hardly
aware of what he was saying, he had moved close to the chest
of drawers without effort, probably as a result of the practice
he had already had in bed, and now he was trying to stand
up straight using it. He actually wanted to open the door.
He really wanted to let himself be seen by and to speak with
the attorney. He was eager to see what the others, who were
making such demands of him, would say once they caught a
glimpse of him. If they were startled, then Gregor had no more

responsibility and could be calm. But if they took in everything quietly, then he would have no reason to get excited and could, if he hurried, actually be at the train station around eight o'clock. At first he slid down a few times on the smooth chest of drawers, but eventually, he gave himself a final swing and stood upright there; he paid no more heed to the pains in his lower body, no matter how they might still sting. Now he let himself fall against the back of a nearby chair, on the edge of which he braced himself with his thin limbs. By doing this, he gained control over himself and kept quiet, for he could now hear the attorney.

"Did you understand even a single word?" the attorney asked the parents. "Is he making a fool of us?" "For God's sake," cried the mother, already in tears. "Perhaps he's very ill, and we're upsetting him. Grete! Grete!" she then cried out. "Mother?" called the sister from the other side. They were communicating through Gregor's room. "You must go to the doctor immediately. Gregor is sick. Hurry to the doctor. Have you heard Gregor speak yet?" "That was an animal's voice,"[18] said the attorney with a voice that was remarkably quiet in comparison to the mother's screaming. "Anna! Anna!" yelled the father through the hall into the kitchen, clapping his hands. "Fetch a locksmith right away!" The two young women ran immediately through the hall with swishing skirts—how had his sister dressed herself so quickly?—and tore open the front door. No one heard the front door close at all; it was left wide open, as is customary in apartments where a huge tragedy has occurred.

Gregor, however, had become much calmer. All right, people did not understand his words any more, although they seemed clear enough to him, clearer than before, perhaps because his ears had become accustomed to them. But at least people now thought that things were not well with him and were prepared to help him. The confidence and assurance with which the first arrangements had been carried out made him feel good. He felt himself included once again in the circle of humanity and was expecting from them both, from the doctor and from the locksmith, without exactly differentiating between them, splendid and surprising results. In order

[18]*Gregor is now unable to talk to other human beings. See glossary note on Communication.*

to get as clear a voice as possible for the decisive discussion to come, he coughed a little, and yet he took pains to ensure that this was muted, since it was possible that even this noise sounded like something different from a human cough, and he no longer trusted himself to discern whether it was or not. Meanwhile, in the next room, it had become completely quiet. Perhaps his parents were sitting with the attorney at the table whispering about him; perhaps they were all leaning against the door, eavesdropping.

Gregor pushed himself slowly towards the door with the help of the chair, let go of it there, threw himself against the door, held himself upright against it—the balls of his tiny legs had a little adhesive on them—and took a brief respite from his labors. But then he took it upon himself to rotate the key in the lock with his mouth. Unfortunately it seemed that he had no real teeth—with what then was he to grab hold of the key? But for this, of course, his jaws were very strong; with their help, he really brought the key into motion, and didn't quite pay attention to the fact that he was undoubtedly causing some harm to himself, because a brown liquid came out of his mouth, flowed over the key, and dripped onto the floor.

"Just listen," said the attorney in the adjacent room; "he's turning the key." This really cheered Gregor up, but they all should have called out to him, including his father and mother; they should have shouted, "Come on, Gregor, get right near it; hold fast to that lock!" Imagining that all his efforts were being followed with suspense, he focused, with all the determination and strength he could summon, on the lock. After each progression of the key's rotation, he danced about the lock; he held himself upright now only with his mouth, and he had to hang onto the key or, as necessary, to press it down once more with the whole weight of his body. The clear noise of the bolt as it finally snapped back positively woke Gregor up. Out of breath, he said to himself: "So I didn't need the locksmith," and he set his head against the door handle to open the door completely.[19]

The door had already been opened wide without him yet being completely visible, seeing that he had had to open it

[19]*Gregor opens the door of his room without relying on anyone else or receiving any aid or encouragement. It is likely that, were the threat of losing his job not hanging over his head, he would have stayed in the room.*

in this way. He first had to turn himself slowly around the edge of the door, very carefully, of course, if he didn't want to fall clumsily on his back right at the entrance into the room. He was still preoccupied with this difficult movement and had no time to pay attention to anything else when he heard the attorney shout out a loud "Oh!"—it sounded like the wind whistling—and now he saw him, the nearest one to the door, pressing his hand against his open mouth and retreating slowly, as if pushed back by an invisible, constant, inexorable force. The mother—she stood here, in spite of the presence of the attorney, with her hair standing on end all over the place from the night—was looking at the father with her hands clasped. She then took two steps towards Gregor and collapsed right in the middle of her skirts, which were spread out all around her; her face was sunk on her breast, completely concealed. The father clenched his fist, showing a hostile expression, as if he wanted to push Gregor back into his room, then looked uncertainly around the living room, covered his eyes with his hands, and cried so that his mighty breast shook.[20]

At this point, Gregor did not take one step into the room, but leaned his body from the inside against the firmly bolted door, so that only half his body was visible, as well as his head, tilted sideways, with which he peeped over at the others. Meanwhile it had become much brighter; standing out clearly from the other side of the street was a part of the endless, gray-black house situated opposite—it was a hospital—with its severe windows regularly spaced across the front; the rain was still coming down, but only in large, individual drops visibly and firmly thrown down one by one onto the ground.[21] The breakfast dishes were sitting in abundant quantities on the table because the father held breakfast to be the most important meal of the day and let it drag on for hours by reading different newspapers. On the wall directly opposite hung a photograph of Gregor from the time of his military service, depicting him as a lieutenant, as if he, with his hand on his fencing sword, smiling and worry free, demanded respect for his bearing and uniform. The door to

[20] *This evidences the father's dual nature. See glossary note on Father.*

[21] *As Kafka words the sentence, the raindrops are an existentialist symbol of immediate, transient existence. See glossary.*

the hall was ajar, and since the door to the apartment was also open, one could see the apartment's landing and the first steps of the staircase leading down beyond.

"Now," said Gregor, well aware that he was the only one who had kept any composure, "I'll promptly get dressed, pack up the collection of samples, and set off. You all want, you all want to allow me to go on my way? You see now, Attorney, sir, I am not stubborn, and I am happy to work; traveling is arduous, but without traveling, I couldn't live. Where are you going, my dear Attorney? To the office? Really? Will you report everything truthfully? A person can be incapable of work momentarily, but that's precisely the time one should remember and consider earlier achievements, so that, after the obstacles have been removed, the person will work that much more industriously. I am completely indebted to the supervisor, and this you know full well. On the other hand, I have to provide for my parents and the sister. I'm in a fix, but I'll work myself out of it again. Don't make things more difficult for me than they already are. Be my advocate in the office! People don't like traveling salesmen, I know. People think you can have a good life only by earning a bundle of money. People don't even have any good reason to stop and think over this prejudice. But you, my dear attorney, you have a better perspective on the circumstances of various people, even, I tell you in total confidence, a better perspective than the supervisor himself, who in his capacity as the employer is hardly bothered when he makes decisions that disadvantage his employees. You also know well enough that the traveling salesman who is away from the office almost the entire year can so easily become a victim of rampant gossip, coincidences, and groundless complaints, against which it's impossible for him to defend himself and most of which he doesn't experience first-hand; and he finds this all out only when he's exhausted after finishing a trip, at home where terrible consequences of unknown origin begin to make themselves felt in his body. Attorney, sir, don't go away without saying one word to me indicating that you think I'm at least partially right!"

But at Gregor's first words, the attorney had already turned away, and now he only looked back at Gregor, pursed his lips and shrugged his shoulders.[22] During Gregor's speech, he was not still for a moment, but kept inching his way towards the door without taking his eyes off Gregor, very gradually, as if there existed some secret ban on leaving the room. He was already in the hall, and given the sudden movement with which he pulled his last foot out of the living room, one could have believed that he had just burned his soles. In the hall, however, he stretched his right hand out away from his body towards the stairs outside, as if a heavenly deliverance were waiting for him there.

Gregor realized that he must not, under any circumstances, allow the attorney to go away with this opinion, especially if his position in the company were not to be placed in the greatest danger. His parents didn't understand this well at all; over the long years, they had built up the conviction that he would be employed for life by this company, and, in addition, they had so much to do nowadays with their present troubles that they had lost all foresight. But Gregor had this foresight. The attorney must be stopped, calmed down, convinced, and finally won over; the future of Gregor and his family depended on it! If only sister had been there! She was clever; she had already cried while Gregor was still lying quietly on his back. And the attorney, this ladies' man,[23] would certainly be tractable for her; she'd have shut the door of the apartment and talked him out of his terror. But the sister wasn't even there; Gregor had to handle it himself. And without considering that he, as of yet, didn't know his current perambulatory abilities, and without thinking that his speech possibly—nay, probably—would still not be understood, he left the door and pushed himself through the opening He wanted to go over to the attorney, who was holding on with both hands to the banister in the forecourt in a completely laughable fashion, but immediately fell, looked for something to stop the fall, and with a weak cry came down upon his many little legs. This had scarcely happened when he felt a sense of physical well-being for the first time that morning; the diminutive legs had a solid floor beneath them; they obeyed perfectly, he noticed to his joy, and even strove to carry him forward where he wanted; he already believed that the immediate alleviation of

[22]*The attorney's indifference further illustrates the existentialist idea that one cannot rely on anyone or anything beyond the individual.*

[23]*The term "ladies' man" (German: Damenfreund) indicates that the attorney might be susceptible to female charms.*

all his hardships was unequivocally before him. But at the very moment when he lay on the floor, rocking back and forth with a repressed motion, quite close and directly across from his mother, she, who appeared so totally lost in her own thoughts, all of a sudden shot up with her arms spread wide and her fingers extended and cried out, "Help, for God's sake, help!" She held her head bowed down, as if she wanted to view Gregor better, and yet in spite of this, she senselessly ran backwards, forgetting that behind her stood the table with all the dishes on it; arriving at the table, she (as if she were absent-minded) sat down hurriedly on it and hardly appeared to notice that near her a stream of coffee was pouring forth onto the carpet from the large, toppled pot.

"Mother, mother," said Gregor quietly, and looked over towards her. The attorney fled momentarily from his mind; on the other hand, he could not keep himself from repeatedly snapping his jaws in the air at the sight of the flowing coffee. At that his mother began her screaming all over again, fled from the table, and collapsed into the arms of his father, who was hurrying towards her. But Gregor had no time right now for his parents; the attorney was already on the stairs; his chin level with the banister, the attorney looked back for the last time. Gregor began sprinting to ensure that he caught up with him as soon as possible; the attorney must have suspected something, because he leapt down multiple steps and disappeared. "Humph!" he then cried, and it rang throughout the entire stairwell.

Unfortunately, it appeared that the attorney's flight had completely bewildered father, who, up to this point, had been relatively composed; instead of running after the attorney or, at the very least, not hindering Gregor in his pursuit, he gripped the attorney's cane, which he had left behind on a stool with his hat and pullover, and with his left hand picked up a large newspaper from the table and attempted to drive Gregor back into his room by stamping his feet and swinging the cane and newspaper. None of Gregor's pleas helped, and no plea was understood; no matter how humbly he hung his head, the father stamped more violently. On the other side of the room, mother had, in spite of the cold weather, thrown open a window, and, leaning out, she put her hands on her face and thrust it far out of the window. A strong draft arose from between the alley and the stairwell; the curtains flew up and the newspapers on the table rustled as individual pages drifted down to the floor.

The father pushed relentlessly forward, hissing like a wild savage. Now Gregor as of yet had hardly any practice going backwards—it really went very slowly. If Gregor had only been allowed to turn around, he would have been in his room immediately, but he feared that father would become impatient with the time-consuming process of turning around, and at every moment, a lethal blow from the cane in the father's hand threatened Gregor's head or back. Eventually, there was really nothing else left for Gregor to do because he realized with horror that he no longer understood how to maintain a direction while going backwards. So he began, while incessantly casting anxious sideways glances at the father, he began to turn himself around as quickly as possible (although in reality, however, this was quite slow). Perhaps father noticed his good intentions, because he did not disturb him as he did this, instead conducting Gregor's rotation here and there from afar with the tip of his stick. If only father weren't making that unbearable hissing noise![24] Gregor was going out of his mind because of this. He was ever at the point of being almost completely turned around, when, because of this hissing, he erred and turned back a bit. When he was finally lucky enough to get his head before the doorway, it became apparent that his body was too wide to go through any further.

It naturally didn't occur to the father, in his present state of mind, to open the second of the two doors, for instance, in order to create a passage of sufficient width for Gregor to go through. He was obsessed with the idea of getting Gregor into his room as quickly as possible. Never would he have stood for the elaborate preparations that Gregor needed to get himself straight and, in this way, to go through the door. Rather, as if there were no obstacles in the way, he drove Gregor forward with an exceptional noise; it hardly sounded to Gregor as if there were one single father behind him—this was really no fun now, and Gregor, come what may, forced himself in the

[24]*The father is depicted as more like an animal than Gregor, especially through the hissing noise.*

door. He raised the one side of his body, and lay on a slant in the doorway; his one flank was rubbed raw, ugly blotches were left on the white door, and soon he was stuck fast, since on his own, he couldn't stir because the little legs on one side were twitching up in the air and, on the other side, were painfully pressed to the floor—then the father came from behind and gave him a truly liberating and hefty push, and he flew, heavily bleeding, far into his room. The door was slammed shut with the cane. It was finally silent.

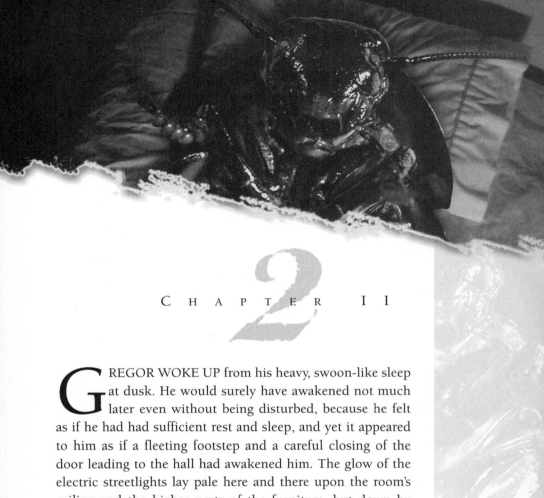

CHAPTER II

GREGOR WOKE UP from his heavy, swoon-like sleep at dusk. He would surely have awakened not much later even without being disturbed, because he felt as if he had had sufficient rest and sleep, and yet it appeared to him as if a fleeting footstep and a careful closing of the door leading to the hall had awakened him. The glow of the electric streetlights lay pale here and there upon the room's ceiling and the higher parts of the furniture, but down by Gregor it was dark. Slowly, he pushed himself to the door, still groping awkwardly with his feelers, which he just now learned to appreciate, so that he could take a look at what was happening there. His left side seemed to be a single, long, unpleasant, stretching scar, and he had to positively limp on his two rows of legs. Moreover, one little leg was severely injured during the course of the morning's incidents—it was a miracle that only one had been injured—and it dragged lifelessly behind.

luckily just one

He first noticed by the door what it was that had tempted him: it had been the smell of something edible. There stood a bowl filled with sweet milk in which swam small bits of white bread. He had almost laughed for joy because he was much more hungry than he had been that morning, and he immediately submerged his head into the milk almost up to his eyes.

can't stand the taste now

his body wasn't helping so he couldn't eat any more

[1]*Many homes still used gas lamps for illumination in the early part of the 20th century.*

But he soon pulled his head back in disappointment, not only because eating was difficult with his delicate left side—he could only eat when his entire body, panting, would assist. Moreover, the milk, which was his favorite drink, and for this reason the sister had certainly prepared it, did not taste good to him at all, and so he writhed away from the bowl in disgust and crawled back to the middle of the room.

In the living room, as Gregor saw through the open door, the gas was lit;[1] during this time of the day, the father was in the habit of reading the afternoon edition of the newspaper in a loud voice to mother and sometimes also to sister, and yet instead, there was silence. Now, perhaps this reading aloud, of which the sister had always told him and wrote to him about, was a custom that, of late, had been entirely abandoned. But it was also just as quiet throughout the apartment, in spite of the fact that it was certainly not empty. "I say, such a quiet life the family leads," said Gregor to himself. As he stared into the darkness in front of him he felt a great pride in the fact that he could have provided such a life in such a nice apartment for his parents and his sister. 1 But what now, if all peace, all prosperity, all contentment should be brought to a frightful end? In order not to lose himself in such thoughts, Gregor, instead, began to move and crawled up and down in his room.

Once, during the long evening, the door on one side and then the other opened slightly, then quickly closed again; someone may have needed to come in, but then had some misgivings about doing so. Now, Gregor immediately stopped crawling near the door, quite determined to somehow bring in the hesitant visitor, or, at the very least, to discover who it is was. But now the door no longer opened, and Gregor waited in vain. Earlier, when the doors had been blockaded, all of them had wanted to come in to him; now that he had opened one door (the other doors had obviously been opened during the day) no one came any more, and the key was now inserted from the outside of the door.[2]

[2]*The word* door *(German: Tür), used seven times in this short paragraph, is symbolic of Gregor's inability to interact with the rest of humanity. See glossary note on* Isolation.

The light in the living room was first turned off late at night, and now it was easy to ascertain that the parents and sister had stayed awake this long because, as one could clearly hear, they were tiptoeing away. Certainly at this point, nobody would come in to Gregor any more until morning. He had a long, uninterrupted time to ponder how he should put his life in order again. But the high, open room in which he was forced to lie flat on the floor made him anxious, and he could not find out the source of his anxiety, because for the past five years, he had inhabited this room. And with a half-unconscious turn and not without a little shame, he hurried under the couch, where he, despite the fact that his back was a little scrunched and despite the fact that he could no longer raise his head, he felt very cozy and regretted only that his body was too wide to fit fully underneath the couch.

There he remained the whole night, part of which he spent dozing, always waking with a start because of his hunger, and another part of which he spent in worry and vague hopes, which all led to the conclusion that he would have to behave quietly for the time being and endure with patience and the greatest consideration for his family the troubles that in his present state he was now suddenly forced to cause them.

In the early morning—it was yet night—Gregor already had the opportunity to test the strength of the carefully-considered resolutions he had made, because the sister, almost fully dressed, opened the door leading to the hall and looked with anticipation inside. She did not find him right away, but as soon as she noticed him under the couch—God, he simply had to be somewhere, he couldn't really fly away—she was so shocked that, without being able to control herself, she shut the door again from the outside. But, as if she rued her behavior, she immediately opened the door again and tiptoed inside, as she would near a seriously ill person or even a stranger. Gregor had pushed his head forward, right to the edge of the couch and observed her. He wondered: Would she really notice that he had let the milk stay there, and not even from a lack of hunger; would she bring in another dish that was more suitable for him? If she didn't do it herself, he would rather starve than to make her aware of this, even though he actually had a gargantuan urge to shoot out from under the couch, throw himself at sister's feet, and beg her to bring anything that was good to eat. But the sister immediately noticed with astonishment that the bowl, out of which only a little milk was spilled round about, was still full; she lifted it up immediately, not with merely her hands but with a rag, and carried it out of the room. Gregor was especially curious about what she would bring in its place, and he thought up various ideas about it. However, he could have never guessed what his sister, out of the kindness of her heart, actually did. She brought him an entire smorgasbord in order to investigate his tastes, all of it spread out on an old newspaper. There were old, half-rotted vegetables; bones from the evening meal that were coated with a congealed white sauce; a few raisins and almonds; a piece of cheese that Gregor had declared to be inedible two days ago; a stale piece of bread, a piece of bread with butter smeared on it, and another piece of bread with butter and salt smeared on it. In addition to all of this, she also put down a bowl (probably intended to be Gregor's for all time) into which she had poured some water. And, out of her tenderness of heart, knowing that Gregor would not eat in front of her, she hurried away, even turning the key in the lock so that Gregor would notice that he might make himself as comfortable as he wanted. Gregor's little legs buzzed now as if they themselves were about to eat. In addition, his wounds must have completely healed already; he felt no handicap any more, and was astonished at this, remembering that he had cut his finger a little with a knife a month ago and that this wound had still hurt the day before yesterday.

"Could I be less sensitive now?" he thought, already sucking greedily on the cheese to which he, over and above the other foods, had immediately and aggressively been drawn. As tears of satisfaction came to his eyes, he consumed the cheese, the vegetables, and the sauce in quick succession. In contrast, the fresh foods didn't taste good to him; he couldn't endure the smell and dragged the things that he wanted to eat a bit further away. He had long been finished with everything and had been lying lazily in the same place for some time when his sister indicated that he should move back by turning the key slowly. This immediately startled him, in spite of the fact that he was almost slumbering, and he hurried once more underneath the sofa. But it required a great amount of will power to remain under the couch, even during the short time during which his sister was in the room, because his body had become a bit round due to the copious food, and he could hardly breathe in the narrow space. As tears poured from his eyes, and in the midst of minor asphyxiation attacks, he looked at his unsuspecting sister as she used a broom to sweep into a bucket, not just the leftovers but also the food that Gregor had hardly touched, as if these were not usable any more; she closed the wooden lid and then carried it all out of the room. She had hardly turned around when Gregor pulled himself out from under the couch, stretched out, and flatulated.[3]

In this manner, Gregor now received his food daily: Once in the morning while the parents and the maid still slept, and a second time after the common lunch, as at that time the parents likewise slept again for a while, and the maid was sent away by his sister to do some shopping. They surely would not have wanted Gregor to starve, but perhaps they couldn't have endured any experience of his eating other than hearsay; or perhaps sister was trying to save them from what was possibly only a small sorrow, as they had actually suffered quite enough already.[4]

Gregor couldn't find out at all with what excuses they had previously sent the doctor and locksmith out of the house that first morning; as he could not be understood by the others, not even sister, nobody thought that he could understand them, and so when the sister was in his room, he had to be content hearing her sighs and appeals to the saints. Only later, when she had grown used to everything—of fully becoming accustomed to it there was never any discussion, of course—did Gregor sometimes manage to hear comments that were meant in a friendly way or could be so construed. "But today, it tasted good to him," she said when Gregor had really put away the food; while in the opposite situation, which gradually began to repeat itself more and more often, she was in the habit of sadly saying, "Now it's all come to a standstill again."

While Gregor could find out no news directly, he did overhear some things from the neighboring room; he ran immediately to the appropriate door and pressed against it

[3] *The German word* blähen *used here means* expand *or* billow *only when referring to curtains or a boat's sail; when related to food or digestion, as it is here, it means to pass gas.*

[4] *The only difficulty that the family has complained about seems to be the loss of Gregor's income and, consequently, the prospect of having to work for a living.*

Grete feeds him scraps daily

with his whole body as soon as he heard voices. There wasn't any conversation (especially in the early days) that didn't somehow concern him, even if it only hinted at it. For two entire days there were discussions at every meal about how they should now go about things; but between mealtimes, they spoke about the same subject because there were always at least two family members at home—nobody really wanted to remain alone in the apartment, and yet, under no circumstances could they entirely abandon it. On that first day, the maid—what and how much about the occurrences she knew was entirely unclear—had also fallen to her knees and begged the mother to dismiss her immediately, and when she said goodbye a quarter of an hour later, she thanked mother for the dismissal with tears, as if it were the greatest favor that anybody had done for her, and, without anyone requesting it of her, swore a terrified oath never to tell anyone the slightest word.[5]

Now, the sister had to cook in conjunction with the mother; this was not a lot of trouble, mind you, because they hardly ate anything. Time and time again, Gregor heard one of them extend to another a futile invitation to eat and receive no other answer than, "Thank you, I've had enough," or something similar. Perhaps they also drank nothing. Sister often asked the father whether he wanted to have a beer and gladly offered to get it herself; when the father remained silent, she said that she would send the doorkeeper to go get it, but then father finally voiced an emphatic "No," and no more was said about it.

During the course of the first day, father had already laid out the entire financial situation and prospects to both mother and sister. Now and then he stood up from the table and took some receipt or ledger out of his small lockbox, saved from the successful collapse[6] of his business five years ago. One could hear as he opened wide the complicated lock and, after removing the sought-after item, locked it again. These declarations of his father were in part the first delightful thing that Gregor had heard during his imprisonment. He had had the impression that the father had nothing at all left from his

[5]*Although the narrator (Kafka) downplays the event, lessening its significance by calling it an "occurrence" (German: der Vorfall) the maid's reaction indicates that she, at least, was traumatized by it.*

[6]*A successful collapse (German: erfolgten Zusammenbruch) is a self-contradictory term indicating that the only thing at which the father succeeded was destroying his business.*

former business, or, at least, father had not said anything to the contrary, and at any rate, Gregor hadn't asked about it. Gregor's only concern had been to do everything in his power to allow his family to forget, as quickly as possible, the bad business luck that had brought them to complete despair. And since that time, he had begun to work with a particular fervor, going almost overnight from being a minor clerk to a traveling salesman, who naturally had a lot of other possibilities for earning money because his success at work was transformed immediately into the form of a cash commission that could be laid on the table at home before his astonished and delighted family.[7]

Those had been fine times, and they had never thereafter been repeated—at least not with the same splendor—despite the fact that Gregor later earned so much money that he was capable of bearing the expenses of the entire family, as he also did. They had become quite used to it, the family as well as Gregor; they accepted the money gratefully, and he gladly handed it over, but it no longer resulted in that special warmth. Only the sister still remained close to Gregor, and his secret plan was to send her, who differed from Gregor in that she loved music and knew how to play the violin movingly, to the conservatory next year, without any consideration for the significant cost that it must entail; they would recoup that in other ways. During Gregor's brief layovers in the city, the conservatory was often mentioned in conversations with the sister, but always as a mere, beautiful dream, the realization of which was unthinkable; the parents never relished listening to the mention of these things, but Gregor had considered it in detail and intended to formally explain his thoughts on Christmas Eve.

In his present circumstances, such useless ideas ran through his head while he adhered to the door and eavesdropped. At times, his general fatigue made it such that he could hardly listen; he carelessly let his head thump against the door, but immediately pulled it back up, as even this little noise that he had caused had been heard in the next room and had silenced them all. "What is he up to now?" said the

[7]*Prior to his metamorphosis, Gregor seems to have worked hard enough to earn large cash commissions, although the attorney indicated earlier that Gregor was not making any sales.*

father after a while, obviously turning towards the door, and only then would the interrupted conversation gradually pick back up again.

Gregor heard quite a few times—the father was in the habit of often repeating his explanations, in part because he had not dealt with these things for a long time now, and in part because the mother did not always understand every-thing correctly the first time—that in spite of all bad luck, a very small fortune from the old times was still available, and in the interim the interest, which had not been touched, had allowed it to sprout and grow. In addition, the money that Gregor had brought home every month—he had only kept a few guilders for himself—had not been completely used up and had accumulated to become a small asset. Gregor nodded eagerly behind his door, delighted at this unexpected foresight and frugality. He would have actually preferred it if they could have further paid off his father's debt to the boss with this sur-plus money so that the day that he could be rid of this position would be much closer, but things were undoubtedly better the way his father had set them up.[8]

Right now, however, this money was entirely insufficient to allow the family to live on the interest; it was perhaps enough to sustain the family for one or at the most two years, but no more. It was simply a sum that one was never really allowed to attenuate and that would have to be put aside for an emer-gency; the money to live on, however, had to be earned. Now, the father was a quite healthy—albeit older—man who hadn't worked at all for five years and in any case couldn't be relied upon too much; he had put on a lot of weight in those five years, which had been the first vacation of his toil-filled and unsuccessful life, and had thus become quite ponderous. And should the old mother now perhaps earn money, she who suffered from asthma, for whom a walk through the apart-ment was strenuous, and who spent every other day on the sofa under an open window because of breathing trouble? And should the sister earn money, she who was yet a child with her seventeen years, whose way of life up to this point was so enviable, consisting of dressing herself nicely, sleep-ing late, helping with household matters, partaking in a few

[8]Undoubtedly better (German: zweifellos besser) Kafka uses the term sarcastically, since it is clear that the family has been taking advantage of Gregor.

modest pleasures, and above all playing the violin? When it came to conversing about the necessity of earning money, the first thing Gregor did was run away from the door and throw himself on the cool leather sofa near the door, as he was very hot with shame and sorrow.

He often lay there all night long, not sleeping a wink and scratching at the leather for hours. Neither did he shy away from the great effort of pushing an armchair to the window, crawling up to the window sill and, propped up on the chair, leaning and looking out the window, obviously with some sort of memory of the freedom he formerly enjoyed. He actually saw, more and more indistinctly from day to day, even things that were not far removed from him. He could no longer catch any glimpse at all of the hospital across the way, the frequent sight of which he had previously cursed, and if he hadn't known for sure that he lived on the quiet yet very urban Charlotte Street, he could have believed that his window overlooked a wilderness in which the gray heavens and the gray earth, indistinguishable from one another, merged. The observant sister needed only to see twice that the stool stood by the window, and then each time that she tidied up the room, she slid the stool back to the same place by the window, from now on even leaving the inner window frame open.

If Gregor could only speak to his sister and thank her for everything that she had to do for him, he would have more easily endured her service; as it stood, however, he suffered through it.[9] The sister sought, of course, to conceal the embarrassment of everything as much as possible, and as more time went by, she naturally got better at doing this—but Gregor was also able to see through all these attempts much better as time went on.[10] Her entrance into the room was already terrible for him. Hardly had she stepped in before she, without taking time to shut the door (even though she generally took great care to spare anyone a view of Gregor's room), ran directly to the window, tore it open in haste almost as if she were suffocating, and remained there breathing deeply for a little while, even when it was still so cold. With this running

[9]*Gregor's suffering is not yet physical. Instead, in the existentialist view, it is a pain caused by isolation, shame, embarrassment, and the angst he feels about his predicament.*

[10]*Here Grete is very hospitable to Gregor. Note her attitude at the end of the book in regards to this.*

[11]*Kafka leaves unanswered the question of which the sister finds more offensive: the way Gregor smells or the smell of the rotten food. See glossary note on Vagueness.*

[12]*Note Kafka's use of a triple negative in the sentence:* would not have thought it unexpected if she had not... *(German: Es wäre für Gregor nicht unerwartet gewesen, wenn sie nicht...)*

and racket, she startled Gregor twice a day; the entire time, he trembled under the couch and knew quite well that she would gladly have spared him all this if it had only been possible to stay with closed windows in a room where Gregor lived.[11]

Once—a full month had already gone by since Gregor's transformation, and the reason for this could hardly be that the sister found herself astounded by Gregor's appearance—she entered a little earlier than usual and came upon Gregor while he was still looking out the window, immobile and situated so as to scare. Gregor would not have been surprised if she had not entered,[12] because his position would have prevented her from opening the window immediately, but she did not only not enter, she retreated immediately and shut the door; a stranger would have thought that Gregor had been lying in wait there and had wanted to bite her. Gregor had immediately hidden himself under the couch, of course, but he had to wait until midday before the sister returned, and she seemed much more nervous than usual. He realized from this that the sight of him was now unbearable even for her and would henceforth remain unbearable for her, and that she would have to force herself not to run away from even the small part of his body that stuck out from underneath the couch. In order to spare her even this sight, he one day dragged the linen sheet onto his back—he needed four hours for this work—and situated it on the couch in such a way that he was now completely concealed, and the sister couldn't see him, even when she bent down. If the linen sheet wasn't necessary, in her opinion, then she could certainly remove it, because it was certainly clear enough that Gregor could have no pleasure in completely shutting himself up; but she left the linen sheet exactly as it was, and Gregor believed that he even caught sight of a look of gratitude once when he lifted the linen sheet a little with his head to have a look at how the sister appraised the new arrangement.

In the first fourteen days, the parents couldn't bring themselves to come in to him, and he often heard how they fully acknowledged his sister's current work, whereas before they had often become angry with the sister because she appeared to them to be a fairly worthless girl. However, now the both of them, the father and the mother, often waited outside Gregor's room while the sister cleaned up in there, and she had hardly come out before she had to tell in exact detail how things looked in the room, what Gregor had eaten, how he had behaved himself this time, and whether, perhaps, she had noticed a slight improvement. Moreover, the mother wanted to visit Gregor relatively soon, but, at first, the father and the sister held her back with sensible reasons that Gregor listened to attentively and of which he fully approved. Later, however, they needed to hold her back forcefully, and when she cried, "Let me in to Gregor; he is my unfortunate son! Don't you understand that I have to go to him?" Then Gregor thought that perhaps it would actually be good if the mother came in—not every day, of course, but perhaps once per week; she understood everything much better than the sister, who, in spite of all her courage, was still just a child and, in the final analysis, had perhaps taken on such a difficult task only out of childish thoughtlessness.[13]

Gregor's wish to see the mother was soon fulfilled. During the day, Gregor didn't want to show himself at the window out of consideration for his parents; he also couldn't crawl on the few square meters of the floor much. It was very hard for him to endure lying down quietly during the night, and food didn't give him even the smallest pleasure any more, so as a diversion, he picked up the habit of crawling back and forth across the walls and ceiling. He especially liked hanging up on the ceiling; it was much different from lying on the floor—one could breathe more freely. A slight undulation moved through the body, and in the almost absent-minded state that Gregor found himself in up above, it could happen that, to his surprise, he let himself go and crashed to the floor. But now, of course, he had his body under much better control than he did previously and didn't hurt himself by such a great fall. The sister noticed immediately the new entertainment that Gregor had found for himself—he left behind traces of his adhesive when he crept here and there—and got the idea of making Gregor's crawling as easy as possible by getting rid of the furniture that impeded him, especially the chest of drawers and the desk. Now she was in no position to do this herself;

[13]*See glossary note on Mother, Sister.*

however, she didn't dare ask the father for help, the maid
would certainly not have helped her—as this almost sixteen-
year-old girl stood by her post courageously since the former
cook's dismissal, but had begged for the privilege of being
allowed to perpetually confine herself to the kitchen, opening
the door only when specifically called—and so the sister had
no choice except to go fetch the mother one time while the
father was absent. The mother drew near with exclamations of
exuberant joy, but fell silent at the door of Gregor's room. First
the sister checked, of course, to see whether everything in the
room was in order; then she let the mother step in. Gregor
had in great haste pulled the linen sheet further down and
in more folds, and the whole of it really looked like a linen
cloth thrown randomly over the couch. This time Gregor
refrained from spying out from under the sheet; he abstained
from seeing his mother this time, and was just happy that she
had even come. "Come on; you can't see him," said the sister,
and, apparently, she led the mother by the hand. Gregor now
listened as the two weak women managed to move the heavy,
old chest of drawers from its place, and, how the whole time
the sister took upon herself the greater part of the work without listening to the warnings of the mother, who feared that
the sister was going to strain herself. This lasted a long time.
After a quarter-of-an-hour's work, the mother said that they
should instead leave the chest of drawers right there—pri-
marily because it was too heavy, and they would not be done
before the father arrived, and, with the chest in the middle
of the room, Gregor's every path would be barricaded—and
secondarily because it was hardly certain that Gregor would
be pleased with the removal of the furniture. For her, the
opposite seemed to be the case: the sight of the empty walls
oppressed her spirits, and why shouldn't Gregor also have this
feeling, being long used to the room's furniture.

"And is it not so," concluded the mother very quietly,
actually almost whispering as if she wanted to avoid having
Gregor (whose exact position she really didn't know) hear
even the sound of her voice, because she was convinced that
he didn't understand the words; "and is it not so, that we, as
it were, are, through the removal of the furniture, signifying

that we are giving up all hope of recovery and are inconsiderately leaving him to himself? I believe that it would be best if we seek to maintain the room in the exact condition that it previously was, so that Gregor, when he returns to us again, will find everything unchanged, thereby being able to forget the intervening time with that much more ease."[14]

Upon hearing the mother's words, Gregor realized that the lack of any direct human conversation, together with the monotonous life among the family, must have, during the course of these last two months, confused his intellect, because he could not otherwise explain to himself how he could earnestly have longed for his room to be emptied. Did he really desire to let the warm room, comfortably furnished with inherited furniture, be transformed into a cave in which he could then freely crawl in all directions without interference, and yet, also at the same time, quickly and completely forget his human past? Was he even now close to forgetting, and was it only the voice of the mother, long unheard, that had roused him? Nothing should be removed; all must remain; he could not do without the beneficial influence of the furniture upon his condition; and if the furniture prevented him from carrying on with his senseless crawling about, then that was no loss—it was rather a great advantage.

Unfortunately, the sister was of another opinion; she had, certainly not without reason, been in the habit of interceding with the parents as an expert witness in matters concerning Gregor, and so the mother's advice to the sister gave her sufficient grounds to carry out the removal not only of the chest of drawers and the desk, the only things that she had first thought of, but also of the entirety of the furniture, with the exception of the indispensable couch. It was not only childish defiance and the unexpected and hard-won self confidence that prompted this demand; on the contrary, she had also observed that Gregor actually needed a lot of room to crawl about, and the furniture, as far as one could see, was of no use whatsoever toward this end. But maybe the enthusiastic spirit of girls her age also played a role, a temperament that sought its own satisfaction at every opportunity, and because of this Grete now let herself be tempted to make Gregor's situation

[14]*Almost as important as the removal of the furniture itself is the fact that Gregor is helpless to prevent it. His reliance on others has increasingly led to his present inability to affect his own fate.*

strips his room

even more infuriatingly terrifying so that she could do even
more for him than she did now. For who besides Grete would
ever dare even once to step into a room where Gregor was the
sole ruler of the empty walls.

And so she did not let the mother dissuade her from her
course of action, and as the mother seemed completely uneasy
and unsure of herself in this room, she soon fell silent and,
with all her strength, helped the sister to get the chest of drawers out of the room. Now after all, Gregor could do without
the chest of drawers in an emergency, but the desk simply
had to stay. And hardly had the women left the room, groan-
ing as they pushed the chest of drawers, before Gregor stuck
his head out from under the couch in order to see how he
could intervene as carefully and scrupulously as possible. But,
unfortunately, who else but the mother should be the first to
return while Grete had stopped and, with arms wide around
the chest of drawers, was swinging it back and forth by herself, naturally, without moving it from its place. The mother,
however, was not accustomed to the sight of Gregor; he could
have made her sick, and so Gregor, startled, ran backwards
to the other end of the couch, but couldn't prevent the linen
sheet from moving forwards a little. That was sufficient to
draw the mother's attention. She hesitated, stood still for a
moment, and then went back to Grete.[15]

Despite Gregor kept saying to himself that nothing out
of the ordinary was happening except a few pieces of furniture being rearranged, it seemed as if he would soon have to
concede that the coming and going of the women, their little
shouts to one another, and the scratching of the furniture on
the floor seemed to him like a great tumult coming closer on
all sides; and, so tightly did he curl up his head and legs and
press his body to the floor that he would inevitably have to say
to himself that he wasn't going to put up with all this any longer. They were clearing out his room, robbing him of everything that he held dear—they had already taken out the chest
of drawers in which were the fretsaw and his other tools. They
were even now loosening the desk that was fastened to the
floor, the desk upon which he had written out his assignments
as a student at the business university, as a student in the city

[15]*The mother and father continue to prefer Grete to Gregor. This preference intensifies until its culmination at the end of the novel.*

school, yes, even as a student in elementary school—he really didn't have any more time to scrutinize the good intentions of the two women, the existence of whom he had moreover quickly forgotten because they were working almost silently due to exhaustion, and one heard only the heavy plodding of their feet.

So he ventured forth (at that moment the women were leaning on the desk so that they could take a breather) and changed directions four times, as he really didn't know what he should save first; then he saw, conspicuously hanging on the otherwise empty wall, the picture of the lady clothed in nothing but fur,[16] and crawled quickly up to it and pressed himself up against the glass that held the picture in place, and it felt good against his hot underbelly. At least nobody would take this picture that Gregor was completely covering up. He twisted his head towards the living room door so that he could watch the women as they returned.

They hadn't given themselves much of a chance to rest and came back soon; Grete had placed her arm around the mother, almost carrying her. "So, what will we take now?" said Grete as she looked around. Then her gaze met Gregor's on the wall. The mother's presence was truly the sole reason she kept her composure; she leaned her face down towards the mother in order to keep her from looking about, and said, although trembling and without thinking, "Come, wouldn't we rather go back to the living room for one more moment?" Grete's intent was clear to Gregor: she wanted to take the mother to safety and then chase him down off the wall. Now, she could just keep on trying! He was sitting on his picture and wasn't handing it over. He would rather jump in Grete's face.

But Grete's words had worried the mother; she stepped to the side, saw the giant brown mark on the flowered wallpaper, and, before she really came to the realization that it was Gregor she saw, she said in a hoarse, shrieking voice, "Oh, God, oh, God!" and, with her arms wide, as if giving everything up, fell on the couch and didn't stir. "Gregor, you..." cried the sister as she raised her fist and shot him an intense glare. These were the first words that she had addressed

[16]*The picture frame is the only object in the room that Gregor himself has made and is, therefore, a symbol of the self-sufficiency that Gregor formerly had.*

directly to him since the transformation. She ran into the neighboring room to get some sort of medicine that could wake the mother from her faint; Gregor wanted to help as well—there was still time to save the picture—he was, however, stuck fast to the glass and had to forcefully tear himself away.[17] He then ran into the nearby room, as if he could give the sister some sort of advice as he had done in the past, but stood there doing nothing behind her while she rummaged around in various little bottles. She was startled when she turned around; a bottle dropped to the floor and shattered; a sliver of glass injured Gregor's face; some acrid medicine spilled on him; Grete now, without delay, took as many little bottles as she could carry and rushed in to the mother with them, shutting the door closed with her foot. Gregor was now cut off from the mother, who was perhaps near death, with him to blame; he was not permitted to open the door as he didn't want to chase away the sister who had to remain with mother; he now had nothing to do except wait, and, plagued by self-reproach and anxiety, he began to crawl; he crawled all over everything: walls, furniture, and ceilings, and when the whole room had just begun to spin around him, he finally fell, in his despair, onto the middle of the large table.

A little time went by as Gregor lay there weakly; everything around him was quiet; perhaps that was a good sign. There was a ring. The girl was locked in her kitchen as a matter of course, and Grete had to go open it. The father had arrived. "What happened?" were his first words; Grete's appearance had really given everything away. Grete answered with a muffled voice, apparently with her face buried in the father's chest: "Mother fainted, but she's better now. Gregor has escaped." "Of course; I've expected that," said the father. "I've always told you that, but you women don't want to hear of it."

It was clear to Gregor that Grete's far-too-short notification had been interpreted to mean something bad and that the father assumed that Gregor had done something vicious and violent. Therefore, Gregor would have to seek to pacify the father because he had neither time nor opportunity to explain. And so he fled to the door of his room and pushed on it, so that the father would see upon entering from the hall that

[17] *The mother's fainting may be not only because of Gregor's appearance, but also because of the odd display of sexuality when he presses himself onto the picture.*

Gregor had every intention of returning to his room at once, that driving him away was unnecessary, and that one needed only to open the door and he would promptly disappear.

But the father was not in the mood to exchange pleasantries. "Ah!" he cried immediately upon entering, sounding as if he were both furious and glad. Gregor pulled his head back from the door and lifted it towards the father. He had never really imagined father the way he now looked; on the other hand, while he had been crawling around in this new fashion, he lately had missed out on the events of the rest of the apartment, not caring about them as he had previously, and he actually should have been prepared to find that circumstances had changed. Nevertheless, nevertheless, wasn't this still father: the same man who had previously been buried in bed from fatigue while Gregor had embarked upon a business trip, who had greeted Gregor upon his return home at night sitting in an armchair in a dressing gown, hardly able to stand up and only raising his arms as a sign of pleasure, and who walked very slowly between Gregor and the mother during the strolls they seldom took together a few Sundays a year and on major holidays, Mother going slowly near him for his sake, always just a little slower, he, bundled up in his old coat, always working his way forward by putting his walking stick down carefully, and, when he wanted to say something, coming to an almost complete standstill and gathering his escort around him?

Now, however, he was standing starkly upright, dressed in a taut blue uniform with gold buttons like the ones servants in banking institutions wore; his prominent double chin expanded above the high, stiff, pleated collar; from underneath the bushy eyebrows a bright, alert, and penetrating gaze came forth from the black eyes; the normally disheveled white hair was meticulously combed down and precisely parted. He flung his hat, upon which a gold monogram (probably of a bank) was set, across the entire room onto the couch and, with the long coattails of his uniform thrown back, went up to Gregor with a determined face and his hands in his pants pockets.

He really didn't know what father intended; at any rate, the father raised his feet unusually high, and Gregor was amazed at the gigantic size of his boot soles. He didn't dwell on that, though, as ever since the first day of his new life, he had surely known that the father considered only the harshest severity appropriate for him. And so he ran away from the father, froze in place when the father stood still, and hurried away further when the father even stirred. In this way they circumnavigated the room several times without anything decisive happening, and as a consequence of the slow tempo of the whole thing, it didn't have the appearance of a pursuit. Because of this, Gregor remained on the floor for the time being, especially as he feared that the father could consider flight up the walls or on the ceiling to be particularly malicious. Regardless, Gregor had to keep telling himself that he wouldn't be able to keep up this running any longer because every time the father took a step, Gregor had to carry out innumerable movements. He already began to noticeably lose his breath, as he had in his former days when his lungs hadn't been quite trustworthy.[18] As he now staggered about to gather his strength for running, he could barely keep his eyes open; in his witlessness, he could hardly think of deliverance through any method other than running, and he had almost forgotten that the walls were available to him, although they were blocked by the painstakingly-carved furniture full of points and pinnacles, when something small that had been lightly tossed flew close beside and rolled in front of him. It was an apple; a second one flew after it. Gregor stood still in terror and further running was useless because the father had decided to bombard him.

He had filled his pockets from the fruit bowl on the credenza, and now, without aiming precisely, threw apple after apple. These small red apples rolled about on the floor as if electrified and bumped against one another. One weakly thrown apple grazed Gregor's back but slid off harmlessly. One direct hit that flew immediately afterward penetrated Gregor's back; Gregor wanted to drag himself a little further, as if the unexpected and unbelievable pain would go away with a change of position, and yet he felt like he was nailed down and stretched out, all his senses being completely confused.[19] Only with his last glance did he see how the door of his room

[18]*Kafka suffered from tuberculosis; this may be an autobiographical reference.*

[19]*The religious symbolism of the apple may refer to Adam and Eve's banishment from Eden and subsequent loss of innocence. See also glossary note on Backbone.*

had been torn open, how the mother ran out in front of the screaming sister (mother was in her underwear because the sister had undressed her to help her breathe more easily when she fainted), and how the mother then ran to the father; on her way to him, her fastened skirts slid one after another to the floor and as she tripped over the skirts, she assaulted the father and threw her arms around him, uniting wholly with him—Gregor's sight then failed him—as she put her hands on the back of the father's head and bade him spare Gregor's life.

① christ-like now?

father misunderstands great + thinks that wife passed out b/c Gregor attacked her.
He throws fruit at him, hitting him with an apple in the back. Mother begs husband to stop.

Part 2: How much of Gregor's humanity remains
family believes differently on what's best for Gregor

Grete cares for him, but can't stand the sight of him

C H A P T E R 3 I I I

GREGOR'S SEVERE WOUND, from which he suffered for over a month—the apple remained in his
flesh as a visible memento because nobody ventured
to remove it—seemed of its own accord to remind the father
that Gregor, despite his present miserable and revolting form,
was a member of the family that one wasn't permitted to treat
like an enemy Instead, with regards to the dictates of family
obligations, swallowing revulsion, one must endure, if nothing else—endure. And now if Gregor, because of his wound,
had, probably forever, lost his mobility and, like an old
invalid, currently needed many, many minutes to cross the
room—crawling up in the air was unthinkable—he received
what, in his opinion, was entirely sufficient compensation for
this worsening of his condition. In the evenings the living
room door, that he only two hours previously had been in the
habit of closely observing, would be opened so that he, lying
in the darkness of his room, could, without being seen from
the living room, see the entire family at the illuminated table[1]
and, to a degree, with their common consent (which had previously been otherwise), listen to their conversation.

It was admittedly not the lively discussion of the earlier
times that Gregor had always thought about longingly in the
small hotel rooms when he, tired, had had to throw himself

*he believes
he deserves
it*

[1]*Gregor is in dark-
ness, while the
family is bathed in
light. See glossary
note on* Family.

on the damp bedding. What went on was now mostly very
quiet. The father fell asleep in his armchair immediately following the evening meal. The mother and sister cautioned one
another to be quiet; the mother, bent down under the light,
sewed lingerie for a fashion boutique; the sister, who had
accepted a position as a saleswoman, studied stenography and
French in the evenings so that sometime later she, perhaps,
would get a better position. Sometimes the father woke up
and, as if he was unaware that he had slept, said to the mother,
"My, you've already been sewing for such a long time!" Then
he immediately fell asleep again, and, fatigued, the mother
and sister smiled with fatigue at one another.

The father refused with a sort of obstinacy to take off his
servant's uniform even at home, and while the sleeping gown
hung uselessly on a coat hook, he slumbered fully clothed in
his place, as if he were always to serve and even here awaited
the voice of his superior. Consequently, the uniform, which
even at first had not been new, lost all semblance of cleanli-
ness, despite the care of the mother and sister, and Gregor,
often all evening long, would look upon the clothing, covered
in stains and with gold buttons that were always polished,
in which the father would quite uncomfortably and yet
peacefully sleep.

As soon as the clock struck ten, the mother tried to wake
the father with quiet words and convince him to go to bed, as
this was no proper place for a sleep that the father, who had
to report to work at six o'clock, especially needed. But in the
obstinacy that had seized him since he became a servant, he
insisted on remaining a while longer at the table, even though
he regularly fell asleep, and only with the greatest effort could
he be moved to exchange the chair for the bed. Regardless of
how many times mother and sister would besiege him with
coaxing, he would slowly shake his head for a quarter hour
with his eyes closed and did not stand up. The mother would
tug his sleeves, speak flattering words in his ear; the sister
would abandon her tasks to help her, but it didn't cut any ice
with the father. He sank even deeper into his armchair. Only
when the two women grabbed him by the underarms would
he open his eyes, look alternately at the mother and sister,

and usually say, "Live and let live. This is the peace of my old age." And, supported by both women, he would laboriously raise himself as if it were an immense burden, allow himself to be led to the door by the women, wave them aside there, and continue on from there while the mother quickly threw down her sewing kit and the sister her quill pen so that they could run after the father and continue to be helpful to him.

Who in this overworked and fatigued family had time to look after Gregor any more than was absolutely necessary? The household shrank ever smaller: the maid was now dismissed, and a big bony servant with white hair flying about her head came in the mornings and evenings to do the hardest work; the mother took care of everything else, in addition to her copious sewing work. It even happened that various pieces of family jewelry, which the mother and the sister had joyously worn when they entertained company or on festive occasions, were sold, as Gregor found out during the general discussion in the evening about the price they had fetched. However, the biggest complaint was always that they could not leave this apartment, which was too large for their current income, because relocating Gregor was inconceivable. But Gregor fully understood that it was not only consideration for him that forestalled a move, because one could easily transport him in a suitable box with a few air holes, but it was much more the complete hopelessness and the thought that they had experienced a stroke of bad luck unlike any known in their entire circle of family and friends.[2]

They now satisfied, in the extreme, the world's expectations of poor people: the father fetched breakfast for minor bank clerks, the mother sacrificed herself for the underwear of strangers, the sister ran to and fro behind the counter according to the customers' orders, but the family's efforts were insufficient. And the wound in Gregor's back began to hurt anew when mother and sister, after they had brought the father to bed, then returned, disregarded their work, came together, and sat cheek-to-cheek as the mother pointed towards Gregor's room and said, "Shut the door, Grete," and, when Gregor was once more in the darkness, the women, mingling their tears or tearless, stared at the table.

[2]*Kafka here uses litotes, a literary device. See glossary.*

Gregor spent the nights and days with hardly any sleep. Sometimes he considered that, the next time the door was opened, he would take up the family's concerns as he once had. In his thoughts once more appeared, after a long time, the boss and the attorney, the superintendents and the apprentices, the blockheaded janitor, two or three friends from other businesses, a cleaning maid at a hotel in the provinces, a fleeting and favorite memory about a saleswoman in a hat shop whom he earnestly and far too slowly had courted—they all appeared intermingled with strangers or people already forgotten, but instead of helping him and his family, they were entirely unapproachable, and he was happy when they disappeared.

But then, he was hardly in the mood to care for his family, filled as he was with blind rage over their negligent care of him; and even though he could not imagine what he had an appetite for, he still made plans about how he could gain entry to the pantry so that he could take, even though he wasn't hungry, what was his due. Without giving any more thought to how they could especially please Gregor, the sister hurriedly shoved any old food she wanted into the room with her foot before she ran in the mornings and middays to the shop, and in the evening, indifferent as to whether the food had perhaps been only tried or—as most often happened—completely untouched, with a swing of the broom, she swept it out. Cleaning out the room, which she now always did in the evening, could hardly be done quicker. Dirt streaks stretched all along the walls; here and there lay balls of dust and filth. At first, Gregor positioned himself in a corner of the room, characteristically dirty, so as to make, as it were, an accusation. But he could have stayed there all week long with no change in the sister's behavior; she saw the filth just as he did, but she had decided to let it alone.[3]

In this manner she, with a new sensitivity that had actually gripped the entire family, vigilantly ensured that the cleaning of Gregor's room remained set aside for her. One time the mother had endeavored to clean Gregor's room completely —a task that she, only after using a few buckets of water, had accomplished. The pervasive dampness had, however,

[3]*As the sister becomes more independent, she is less inclined to provide for Gregor.*

sickened Gregor and he lay flat, embittered, and immobile on the couch—but the punishment for the mother was yet to come. In the evening, the sister had hardly noticed the change before she, highly offended, ran into the living room and, despite the pleading hands raised by the mother, broke out into fit of crying that the parents—the father was naturally shocked out of his armchair—first looked at with helpless astonishment until they became provoked. On his right side the father began to reproach the mother, telling her not to usurp the cleaning of Gregor's room from the sister and then turned to his left and screamed at the sister, telling her that she may never clean Gregor's room again, while the mother sought to drag the father, beside himself with exasperation, into the bedroom; the sister, shaken by her sobs, worked at the table with her small fists, and Gregor hissed loudly in rage because it hadn't occurred to anyone to shut the door and spare him this scene and commotion.[4]

But if the sister, exhausted from her job and fed up with it as she was, had cared for Gregor herself, the mother would not have had any cause for entering, and Gregor would not have been neglected. That's why the servant was now there. This old widow, who, come what may, had, during her long life, survived even the greatest of troubles with the help of her bony build, had no particular aversion to Gregor. Without being curious, if this were possible, she chanced to open the door of Gregor's room one time and caught a glimpse of Gregor, who, entirely surprised and despite nobody chasing him, began to run to and fro; she, her hands falling into her lap, remained standing there in astonishment. Since then, she never failed to open the door a crack in the mornings and evenings and quickly look in on Gregor. In the beginning she also called out to him with words that she probably thought were friendly, like, "C'mon over here, y'a old dung beetle!" or "Lookie here at the old dung beetle!"[5] Upon being spoken to in such a manner, Gregor did not answer, but instead remained stationary in his place, as if the door hadn't been opened at all. If they had only, instead of letting this servant squander his time by bothering him whenever she was in the mood, commanded her to clean his room every day! Once

[4]*Gregor now wants the door shut; before he had longed to have it open. Note that he now hisses as the father had done earlier. See glossary note on Isolation.*

[5]*This servant is uneducated and speaks colloquial (German: "Komm mal herüber, alter Mistkäfer!").*

in the early morning—a driving rain, perhaps already a sign of the coming spring, pummeled the window panes—as the servant began once more to use her particular form of conversation, Gregor was so bitter that he, as if preparing for an attack—and yet slowly and feebly—turned himself towards her. The servant, however, instead of fearing him, simply lifted high a stool found near the door and stood there with a wide-open mouth. Her intention was clear: to shut her mouth only when the chair in her hand had been slammed down on Gregor's back. "So, this won't go any further?" she asked as Gregor turned himself about again, and she calmly put the chair back in the corner.[6]

Gregor now ate almost nothing. Only when he happened to pass by the prepared food did he, as a game, take a bite in his mouth, hold it there for hours, and then spit most of it out again. At first, he thought that it was dejection over the state of his room that prevented him from eating, but he became reconciled to the room's changes very quickly. They had become accustomed to putting things in this room that they couldn't put elsewhere, and there were now many such things because they had rented out a room of the apartment to three tenants.[7] These stern gentlemen—all three had full beards, as Gregor had once been able to ascertain by looking when the door was opened a crack—were meticulously tidy, not only in their own room, but also, now that they had lodged here, in the entire household (especially in the kitchen). They didn't tolerate things that were useless or just dirty. In addition, they had, for the most part, brought their own furniture with them. For this reason, there were many things that had become superfluous; they really weren't saleable, and yet the family also wouldn't throw them out. All these things found their way into Gregor's room. There was even the box of ashes from the oven and the trashcan from the kitchen. Whatever was useless at present, the servant, who was always in a great hurry, simply hurled into Gregor's room; fortunately, Gregor, for the most part, saw only the item and the hand that held it. Perhaps the servant had the intention either to take out the items when she had the time and opportunity or to throw everything out at once; but, in actuality, the items remained

[6]The new maid also takes part in the continued emasculation of Gregor.

[7]These three tenants are an odd trio, behaving almost like one organism. See glossary note on Tenants.

there where they had first been thrown—except when Gregor wriggled through the junk pile and moved it, at first compelled to do so because there was no longer any free space to crawl, but later with growing pleasure, even though after such romping about, he was tired to the point of death and miserable as he sat for hours without moving.

Because the tenants sometimes also took their evening meal in the common room, the door to the room remained closed some evenings; Gregor quite easily refrained from opening the door, and often didn't take advantage of it when the door was opened some evenings, instead lying down in a dark corner of his room without the family noticing. One time, however, the servant had left the door to the living room open a little, and it remained open this far even when the tenants entered in the evening and turned the lights on. They sat down at the head of the table, where in former times, the father, the mother, and Gregor had eaten, unfolded their napkins, and took knives and forks into their hands. The mother immediately appeared in the door with a dish of meat, and, directly behind her, the sister with a dish stacked high with potatoes. Heavy steam rose from the food. The tenants bent down over the dishes set before them as if they wanted to examine it before eating, and the one sitting in the middle actually cut a piece of meat on the plate—the other two appearing to be regarded as authorities on the matter—obviously to determine whether it was tender enough or whether something should be sent back to the kitchen. He was satisfied, and mother and sister, who had looked on in suspense, heaved a sigh of relief and smiled.

The family itself ate in the kitchen. Despite this, the father, prior to going into the kitchen, came into the room and, hat in hand, made a circuit around the table. The tenants all rose and muttered something in their beards. Then, when they were alone, they ate in almost complete silence. It seemed strange to Gregor that, of all the myriad sounds of eating, it was always the noise of their chewing teeth that Gregor detected, as if, by this, it should be signified to him that one needed teeth to eat, and that even the finest toothless jaw was insufficient for the task. "I really have an appetite," said

Gregor as he worried, "but not for these things. How these tenants nourish themselves while I pass away!"[8]

On this selfsame evening, the violin—Gregor didn't recall having heard it during this whole time—sounded from the kitchen. The tenants had already finished their evening meal; the middle one had produced a newspaper and set it before him; the two others had each received one page, and they now read while they leaned back and smoked. As the violin began to play, they were attentive; they rose and went on tiptoe to the hall door, where they remained standing up against one another. The family must have been able to hear the tenants from the kitchen, because the father called: "Is the playing perhaps unpleasant for the gentlemen? It will be called off at once." "On the contrary," said the gentleman in the middle, "wouldn't the young lady like to come in here to us and play in here, where it is much more comfortable and cozy?" "As you please," cried the father, as if he were the violinist. The gentlemen stepped back into the room and waited. Soon the father came with the music stand, the mother with the music, and the sister with the violin. The sister calmly prepared everything so that she could perform; the parents, who had never before rented a room out and as a result were excessively polite towards the tenants, did not dare in any way to sit on their own chairs; the father leaned on the door, with his right hand between two buttons on the the pleats of his livery,[9] but the mother accepted a chair offered by one of the gentlemen and sat where the gentleman had happened to placed the stool, that is, off in a remote corner.

The sister began to play; the mother and father each from their side followed the movements of her hands with their eyes. Gregor, drawn by the playing, had risked coming forward a little bit more; his head was already in the living room. He hardly wondered at the fact that he had recently had so little consideration for the others; earlier, he had been quite proud of this solicitude. He would have had much more reason right now to hide himself, as the dust that lay over the whole of his room and which flew about at the slightest movement now covered him completely as well; he dragged threads, hair, and food scraps with him on his back and sides; he was far

[8]*Gregor is obviously fore-shadowing his own death. See glossary.*

[9]*The father's cloth-ing is an indicator of his social and philosophical sta-tus. See glossary note on* Father.

too indifferent about everything to lay on his back and rub himself on the carpet as he used to do multiple times during the day. In spite of these circumstances, he had no inhibitions about moving forward a little bit over the immaculate floor of the living room. /

At any rate, nobody paid any attention to him. The family was completely engrossed by the violin playing; the tenants, on the other hand, who had placed themselves behind the music stand (far too close behind the sister) so that they could see all of the musical notes, must have disturbed the sister, and soon drew near the window, bowing their heads and speaking in low tones with one another, where they remained as the father anxiously observed them. It quite clearly appeared as if they were disappointed in their assumption that they were going to hear a beautiful or entertaining violin performance, had had quite enough of the entire presentation, and now allowed themselves to be disturbed only out of politeness. The way that they all blew the smoke of their cigars up in the air out of their noses and mouths especially brought one to the conclusion that they were rather annoyed. All the same, his sister was playing so beautifully. Her face was turned to the side, and her gaze, scrutinizing and full of sadness, followed the lines of notes. Gregor crawled a little bit further forwards and held his head close to the floor in order to meet her gaze, if possible. Was he an animal, that music would so move him?[10] It was as if the way to the unknown nourishment that he longed for was shown to him. He was determined to get as far as the sister, to tug at her skirts, and thereby to express that he would like her to come into his room with her violin, as nobody here thought that her playing was worth their time (although he thought it was worthwhile). He did not want to let her out of his room, at least not as long as he lived; his terrifying form should for the first time be useful as he would hiss back at the attackers from all doors of his room at once...and yet the sister shouldn't be forced to stay with him, but instead, remain of her own free will: she should sit near him on the couch, bend her ear down to him, and he would then confide to her that he had every intention of sending her to the conservatory and that, if this

[10]*This is a rhetorical question: Gregor is an animal.*

unfortunate event had not happened in the interim, he would have told her all this last Christmas—Christmas had already gone by?—without listening to any contrary arguments. After this clarification, the sister would erupt in a fit of emotional tears, and Gregor would lift himself up to her shoulders and kiss her throat, which she had left uncovered without a band or collar since she started going to work.[11]

"Mr. Samsa!" cried the tenant in the middle to the father as he pointed, without speaking another word, with his index finger at Gregor, who was moving himself slowly forward. The violin fell silent as the tenant in the middle smiled at his friends and, shaking his head once, looked at Gregor again. The father appeared to consider it more important to calm the tenants than to drive away Gregor, despite the fact that the tenants were hardly upset and that Gregor entertained them more than the violin performance. He hurried to them and sought with open arms to force them back into their room, while, at the same time, trying to obstruct their view of Gregor with his body. They were actually a little angry at this point, although one no longer knew whether it was due to the father's conduct or whether it was the fact that they just now realized that they possessed a neighbor such as Gregor in the next room. They requested explanations from the father, raised their hands, pulled at their beards in restlessness, and retreated to their rooms only slowly. Meanwhile the sister, initially feeling quite lost after the sudden disruption and disintegration of the performance, letting her hands hang motionless with the violin and bow while she had looked at the music as if she were still playing, had overcome her confusion and had laid the instrument on the lap of the mother (who had sat down on her chair because she was short of breath); the sister then ran into the neighboring room, which the tenants were quickly approaching because of the father's pressure. One could see how, under the sister's proficient hands, the sheets and pillows from the bed flew into the air and arranged themselves. Before the gentleman had even reached the room, she was finished with the bedcovers and had slipped out. The father appeared once again to have been seized by his stubbornness, as he forgot every courtesy that he owed his tenants; he pushed forward

[11]*In the beginning of the 20th century, a woman's neck was generally covered by a collar or scarf as a matter of modesty. See glossary note on* Mother, Sister.

and pushed again, until the middle gentleman, already in the door, stamped his foot with a crash and thereby brought the father to a halt. "I hereby declare," said the tenant, raising his hand and searching out the mother and sister as well with his gaze, "that upon consideration of the revolting conditions"—at this he spat resolutely on the floor—"that prevail among this family and in this apartment, I am giving notice of the immediate termination of my occupancy. I will, of course, pay not even the least amount for the days I have lived here; on the contrary, I will contemplate whether or not I will file against you some sort of plea, which—believe me—will be substantiated very easily." He then became silent and looked directly in front of him as if he expected something. Actually, his two friends chimed in with the words: "We also immediately give our notice." Upon that, the middle one grabbed the door handle and slammed the door shut.

The father fumbled about with his hands, staggered to his chair, and fell into it; he looked as if he were stretching out for his usual evening nap, but the way his head deeply nodded, as if totally slack, indicated that he could hardly be sleeping. Gregor had been lying still at the same spot where the tenants had caught him. He was too weak to move because of his disappointment over the fact that his plans had gone awry; he was also weak, possibly as a result of his extreme hunger. He feared, in the next few moments, that it was positively certain that everything would flare up and collapse upon him, and he waited. He wasn't even startled when the violin, held by the mother's trembling hands, fell from her lap and sent out a sonorous tone.

"Dearest parents," said the sister as she struck the table with her hand as an introduction, "this can go no further. If you perhaps don't recognize that, I recognize it. I will not pronounce the name of my brother in the presence of this monster, and will say merely this about it: we must be rid of it.[12] We have attempted every method humanly possible to serve and tolerate it, and I believe that nobody can blame us in the least." "She is a thousand times right," interjected the father. The mother, who could never manage to catch her breath, had a maniacal look in her eyes as she held her

[12]*The sister employs the pronoun it, (German: es or ihm, depending on case) finally referring to Gregor as an animal rather than a person.*

hand up and began to muffle her coughs. The sister hurried
to mother and felt her forehead. The father appeared to have
been lead to contemplate certain things by the sister's words;
he sat upright, played with his servant's cap between the plates
that the tenants had left on the table from the evening meal,
and looked from time to time at the motionless Gregor.

"We must try to get rid of it," the sister now said exclu-
sively to the father because the mother, in her coughing,
heard nothing. "It's doing both of you in; I can see it coming.
If people have to work as hard as we all do, they can't endure
this endless torment at home as well. I can't do it either." And
she burst into tears that were so strong that they flowed down
onto the mother's face, from which the sister wiped the tears
with mechanical motions of her hands.[13]

"Child," said the father with compassion and obvious sym-
pathy, "what then should we do?"

The sister just shrugged her shoulders as a sign of the help-
lessness that, in contrast to her former sureness, had seized
her while she cried.

"If he understood us," said the father half-questioningly;
the sister, in her tears, shook her hand fiercely to signify that
this was unthinkable.

"If he understood us," repeated the father, who, by shutting his eyes, admitted to the sister's conviction regarding the
impossibility of the matter, "then it might be possible to come
to an agreement with him. But as it stands..."

"He must be sent away," cried the sister; "that is the only
way. You just have to try to banish the thought that it's Gregor.
The fact that we have believed this for so long is our true
misfortune. How can it really be Gregor? If it were Gregor, he
would have long recognized that it isn't possible for humans
to live together with such a beast and would have gone away
of his own free will. Then we would have had no brother, but
would have lived our lives and honored his memory. But this
animal persecutes us, drives away the tenants, and evidently
will occupy the entire apartment and let us spend the night
in the alleyway. See, father," she suddenly screamed, "he's
starting again now!" And, with a horror that Gregor couldn't
understand at all, the sister even abandoned the mother,

suddenly pushing away from her chair as if she would rather sacrifice the mother than remain in Gregor's presence, and hurried behind the father, who, only worked up because of her behavior, also stood up and half-raised his arms as if to protect the sister.

But Gregor hadn't any ideas or intentions of causing anxiety for anyone, let alone his sister. He had just started to turn himself around so that he could wander back into his room, and this actually looked quite strange, as he, in his wounded condition, had to facilitate his difficult rotation by raising and then dropping his head many times on the floor. He stopped and looked around. His good intentions seemed to have been recognized; the horror had only been temporary. Now they all silently and sorrowfully looked at him. The mother, with her legs crossed and stretched out in front of her, sat in her chair, with her eyes almost shut from exhaustion; the father and the sister sat near one another, with the sister having laid her hand around the father's neck.[14]

"Now, maybe I'll be allowed to turn myself around," thought Gregor as he began his work once more. He couldn't suppress his wheezing at the effort and had to rest now and then.

In addition, nobody was urging him onwards; it was all left up to him. When he had finished turning around, he immediately began to traipse directly back. He was amazed at the great distance separating him from his room, and he could hardly comprehend how he, in his weakness and almost without noticeable effort, had traced the same path only a short time ago. Concentrating the whole time on crawling quickly, he hardly paid attention to the fact that no word, no cry from his family disrupted him.

He first turned his head when he was already in the door, although he didn't turn it fully because he felt his neck getting stiff; at any rate, he saw that even now nothing behind him had changed, except that the sister was standing up. He last glanced fleetingly at the mother, who was now completely asleep. He was hardly inside his room when the door was swiftly shut, bolted, and locked. Gregor was so startled at the sudden noise behind him that his little legs buckled. It was

[14]*The sister is now lavishing the attention that Gregor needs upon the father.*

the sister who had hurried like that. She already stood upright and had then waited, quickly springing forward (Gregor hadn't even heard her coming), calling out "Finally!" to the parents while she turned the key in the lock.

"And now?" Gregor asked himself as he looked around in the darkness. He soon made the discovery that he could no longer even budge. He wasn't too amazed at this; it actually seemed unnatural to him that, until now, he could actually get around with these thin little legs. Moreover, he felt relatively comfortable. It was true that his whole body hurt, but it seemed to him as if the pains gradually grew slighter and slighter and that they would eventually go away completely. He now hardly felt the rotten apple in his back and the inflammation around it, which was now covered in soft dust. He remembered his family with affection and love. His opinion of it all, which was that he had to disappear, was even more resolute than his sister's, if such a thing were possible. He stayed in this state of vapid and peaceful contemplation until the clock tower struck the third hour of the morning.[15] He lived to see the beginning of the general illumination outside the window. Then, apart from his will, his head sank down completely, and his last breath streamed weakly out of his nostrils.

In the early morning the servant came—with sheer strength and speed she slammed shut all the doors in just the way that they had previously requested she avoid, and so her coming made quiet sleep in the apartment no longer possible—and at her customary short visit with Gregor, she initially found nothing exceptional. She thought he was lying there intentionally motionless, trying to play the insulted victim; she believed him capable of all sorts of intrigues. Since she happened to have the long broom in hand, she tried to tickle Gregor with it from the doorway. When this also failed to produce results, she was annoyed and poked Gregor gently, and only when she had shoved him from his place without any opposition did it draw her attention. When she soon recognized what had actually happened, her eyes grew large, she let out a low whistle, and, not waiting long, she tore open the door of the bedroom and called out in a loud voice into the

[15]*Gregor's death scene is rife with religious references. See glossary.*

Handwritten marginalia:

✱ SA quote

- biblical significance (apple 3rd hour) chrst's death parallel b/c he loves his family but has to disappear.

analagous way is that Gregor could be seen as Christ

- intended to be seen as a new man free from religion & constraints of family

✱ gregor's motivation to die for the sake of his family

- he doesn't fight death b/c he knows its for the best

his death 3rd hr of morning

points to authors existentialist → belief that the individual is a free agent w/ his own choices & decisions

darkness: "Everybody check it out, it croaked; there it lies, it's a stiff!"[16]

The married Samsa couple sat upright in their marriage bed and had to force themselves to overcome their fright of the servant before they understood her announcement. Then, however, Mr. and Mrs. Samsa rapidly climbed out of bed, both on their own side; Mr. Samsa threw the bedcovers over his shoulder, Mrs. Samsa came out only in her gown, and so they entered Gregor's room. In the meantime, the door of the living room, where Grete had slept since the tenants had departed, was also opened; Grete was fully clothed as if she hadn't slept at all, a fact to which her pale face also seemed to attest. "Dead?" said Mrs. Samsa, and she cast a questioning look at the servant, in spite of the fact that she could still examine everything herself and could understand what had happened even without examination. "That's what I think," said the servant who, to prove it, shoved Gregor's body a fair distance to the side. Mrs. Samsa moved forward as if she wanted to stop the broom, but she didn't. "At last," said Mr. Samsa, "now we can thank God." He crossed himself, and the three women followed suit.

Grete, who hadn't taken her eyes off the corpse, said: "Just look at how emaciated he was. He hadn't eaten in such a long time. The food came out of here exactly as it had come in." Gregor's corpse was actually extremely flat and dry, and one really began to notice it only now because he wasn't raised on those little legs, and no other distractions existed.

"Come in here with us for a little while, Grete," said Mrs. Samsa with a melancholy smile, and Grete went behind the parents into the bedroom, although not without looking back at the corpse. The servant shut the door and opened wide the window. Even though it was early morning, the air was fresh and mildly warm. It was already the end of March.

The three tenants stepped out of their room and looked in surprise for their breakfast; they had been forgotten. "Where is the breakfast?" the middle gentleman asked of the servant sullenly. She, however, put her finger to her lips and quickly and silently waved to the gentlemen that they should come

[16]*The servant's slang (German: "Es ist krepiert") is comparable in tone to the American idioms "kicked the bucket" or "bought the farm."*

in Gregor's room. They also came and stood, with their hands in the pockets of their somewhat worn little jackets, around Gregor's corpse in the room that had already become bright.

Then the door of the bedroom opened and Mr. Samsa appeared in his livery; on one arm was his wife, and on the other, his daughter. They were all a little tear-stained; Grete hid her face from time to time on the father's arm.

"Get out of my apartment immediately!" said Mr. Samsa as he pointed at the door without letting go of the women. "How exactly do you mean that?" said the middle gentleman, somewhat shaken and smiling sweetly. The other two kept their hands behind their backs and kept rubbing them against one another as if in gleeful anticipation of a significant argument that would, in any event, turn out to be good for them. "I mean it exactly as I have said it," answered Mr. Samsa as he went in a straight line with his two female escorts to the tenants. They at first stood still and looked at the floor, as if things inside their head were rearranging themselves. "Then we will go," he then said, looking at Mr. Samsa as if, suddenly overcome by humility, he desired further approval for even this resolution. Mr. Samsa only nodded to him curtly several times with wide eyes.

At this, the gentleman immediately went, with long strides, to the hall; his two friends had already been listening for a while with motionless hands and now hopped directly after him, as if worried that Mr. Samsa could step into the hallway before they did and interfere when they joined up with their leader. All three of them took their hats from the coat rack in the hall, took their canes from the cane holder, bowed silently, and quit the apartment. In what turned out to be completely groundless suspicion, Mr. Samsa and the two women stepped out on the porch, leaned on the railing, and watched as the three gentlemen descended the stairs very slowly but surely, disappeared at every floor where the stairs turned, and after a few moments came out once again. The deeper they managed to go, the more the Samsa family lost interest in them, and when a butcher's apprentice walked proudly to them and then went high above their heads on the stairs with a basket[17] on his head, Mr. Samsa and the two women deserted the railing, turned around, and then all, as if relieved, went back into the apartment.

They decided that day to spend time relaxing and going for a walk; not only had they earned this break from work, but they absolutely needed it. And so they sat at the table and wrote three letters of excuse, Mr. Samsa to his manager, Mrs. Samsa to her customer, and Grete to her supervisor at the store. While they were writing, the servant came in to say that she was leaving because her morning work was done. The three writers at first just nodded without looking up, and only when the servant would still not go away, did they look up in annoyance. "Well?" asked Mr. Samsa. The servant stood smiling in the doorway, as if she had something auspicious to announce but would do so only if she were specifically asked about it. The small ostrich feather in her hat which was not quite upright (and which had annoyed Mr. Samsa during the entire time she served them) swayed gently in all directions. "Well then, what is it you actually want?" asked Mrs. Samsa, whom the servant usually respected. "Ahem," answered the servant, who couldn't continue speaking right then because she stood there cheerfully smiling. "Okay, so, about that trash that needed to be gotten rid of, you guys don't worry about that. It's done taken care of."[18] Mrs. Samsa and Grete bent down over their letters as if they wanted to continue writing; Mr. Samsa, who noticed that the servant now wanted to begin describing everything explicitly, promptly nipped that in the bud with an outstretched hand. When she wasn't allowed to narrate, she remembered what a great hurry she was in, and, obviously insulted, called out "Adjoo,[19] folks," turned around fiercely, and left the apartment with a violent slamming of the door.

"She'll be let go this evening," said Mr. Samsa, who received neither from his wife nor daughter any reply because it appeared that the servant had disrupted the tranquility that they had just gained once again. They rose, went to the window, and remained there with their arms around each other. Mr. Samsa turned his chair in their direction and observed them quietly for a little while. Then he called: "Come now. Let's finally put aside the old things. And let's also have a little consideration for me." The women obeyed

[18] *A lower-class stranger takes care of Gregor's body instead of the family, which adds the final insult to his existence.*

[19] *The servant is trying to say the French word adieu (German: adjers), but she has obviously never learned to speak French and mangles the word quite badly.*

him immediately, hastened to him, caressed him, and quickly concluded their letters.

Then all three of them left the apartment together (something that they had not done in months) and took the tram into the open air of the city. Warm sunshine permeated the car in which they all sat. They discussed with one another their prospects for the future as they leaned back comfortably in their seats, and found upon closer examination that they were by no means bad, as the employment of all three of them, which they had not previously asked each other about at all, was favorable and (especially in the future) looked very promising. The most notable immediate improvement of their situation would arise from a change of apartments; they now wanted to take one that was smaller, cheaper, in a better location, and, most importantly, was more practical than their current one that had been chosen by Gregor. As they talked pleasantly about these things, it occurred to Mr. and Mrs. Samsa almost at the same time that their daughter, despite all the recent difficulties that had made her cheeks pale, was growing livelier all the time and had blossomed to become a beautiful and voluptuous young woman. Growing quieter, they almost unconsciously communicated with each other through their glances, thinking that it was soon going to be time to look for a worthy man for her. And it was like a confirmation of their new dreams and good intentions when, as they reached their destination of their trip, the daughter rose up first and stretched her young body.[20]

[20]*The family is once again illuminated, and Grete's stretching indicates that she has fully matured. See glossary on Gregor's Death.*

Glossary

Backbone

The *backbone* in this story is also a symbol of the human ability to remain upright and to determine one's own destiny. As a traveling salesman, Gregor was figuratively spineless, but now that he is a bug, it is a physical actuality. Note also that the apple thrown by the father sticks in Gregor's back, making him even more spineless.

Communication

It becomes apparent at one point in the text that Gregor suddenly cannot communicate with other human beings. This inability is one trait that cuts him off from his family and the rest of the humans in the story. Existentialists generally agree that their beliefs isolate them from other people, making communication difficult.

Father

The father frequently displays his dual nature: he tries to put on a show of strength, but in reality, he is almost as weak as the mother. He is imposingly large, as was Kafka's own father, but is emotionally unable to maturely cope with the new Gregor. His father's clothing is at one point called a *uniform* (German: *die Uniform*) but later is referred to as *livery* (German: *Livreerokkes*), an antiquated word that recalls the clothing a medieval serf worn while serving his or her master.

Also note that Kafka almost always uses the pronoun *the* instead of *his* when referring to Gregor's family (*the father* instead of *his father* or *Gregor's father*). This word choice isolates Gregor even further from his family by subtly implying that he is not intimately associated with them.

Fretsaw

There is little in the novel to show that Gregor has done anything with his fretsaw other than create the ornate frame for the picture of the woman. The mother states at one point that this is his only hobby, which indicates that Gregor has few or no interests outside work. The one object to which he pays attention is the picture of the woman cut from a magazine, which he has put in the frame that he had spent a great deal of time creating.

Gregor's Death

Gregor's death at the end of the book is foreshadowed throughout the novel. At one point, Gregor is proud of the fact that he had previously been capable of providing for the needs of his family, but then is described as *looking into the darkness in front of him*, which may foreshadow his death. Many details of Gregor's death also carry religious overtones or references. The time of his death, *third hour of the morning* (German: *die dritte Morgenstunde*), is not "three o'clock a.m.," which would be *drei Uhr am Morgen* in German, and is possibly a reference to the time of Jesus' crucifixion.

The fact that *illumination* (German: *das Hellerwerden*) begins as Gregor dies is further evidence of this religious correlation. Note that at the end of the story, the members of the family have succeeded in sloughing off their previous lives and are now basking in light and comfort. The major objection to Gregor's state—his inability to provide financial support—has been removed. The family has also managed to erase Gregor from their memories by deciding to move, and at the end, the parents focus solely on the young, pure daughter and her bright future; it is as if Gregor sacrificed himself so that she could succeed.

Gregor's Decision

Gregor makes a decision about his condition: instead of trying to find a way to reverse his transformation, he passively waits for it to go away on its own. This element of existentialism—that there is no common element of humanity and that each person must essentially create his or her own self-existence—is crucial to understanding Gregor Samsa's acceptance of his situation.

Harem Women

When Gregor references "harem women," he mistakenly alludes to the luxurious lifestyle he assumes a harem woman enjoys and indicates that other traveling salesmen enjoy quite a bit of comfort and have the freedom to do as they please. The irony, however, lies in the fact that being a concubine in a harem is not a dignified position, and harem women are certainly not free; they are generally there to do the bidding of a master and would be considered almost slaves. Gregor, in describing his employment status and voicing his complaints, is saying that "harem women" enjoy more independence than he does because his supervisor closely watches his every move.

Isolation

Gregor had been in control of his relationships with others previously, when his doors were locked from the inside. When the keys are inserted from the outside, he is isolated, powerless, dependent upon others, and unable to alter his situation.

Litotes

Litotesis is a literary device that uses understatement to emphasize something. When Kafka calls Gregor's transformation a *stroke of bad luck* (German: *ein großes Unglück*) he lessens and understates the event's significance by saying that it was unknown among all Gregor's family and friends; in reality, it is an event unprecedented in human history.

Mechanical Hand Motions

The sister's hand movements are *mechanical* (German: *mechanischen Handbewegungen*) either because she has had so much practice wiping tears from the mother's eyes that the action is now automatic or because Grete is merely going through the motions. This wording may indicate that her concern for the mother is only a show and that she really doesn't care for her parents.

Metamorphosis

The German title of Kafka's work is actually *Die Verwandlung*, which, directly translated, means *The Transformation*. The first English translations of the book named it *The Metamorphosis*, and it has been called this ever since. Although *metamorphosis* has relevance to the story because it is a type of change that some insects undergo, the German word for this change (*die Metamorphose*) is not what Kafka actually titled the book.

Mother, Sister

Besides Gregor's predatory *lying in wait* (German: *Gregor habe ihr aufgelauert*) for his sister, he also wants his mother (unaccompanied by his father) to come into his bedroom. This hints at an unexplained and ambiguous desire for his mother and sister, along with a sort of jealousy between the father and Gregor. The sister also has a sexual maturity that continues to develop until the end of the novel, evidenced by instances like her uncovered neck (which Gregor wants to kiss) and the stretching of her body.

One

In English, we seldom use the pronoun *one* (as in "One needs to go to the store if one wants to buy bread.") We use the pronoun *you* to talk about people in general. Kafka employs the pronoun *one* quite often. The effect of this linguistic convention is that it removes the characters in the book from the actions and events around them and distances the reader emotionally from the story, and reinforces a formal tone.

Pest / Vermin

It is not until early in Chapter III, when the servant calls Gregor a *dung beetle* (German: *Mistkäfer*) that Kafka gives a more specific idea about what sort of *pest* Gregor has become. There are some descriptive clues in Chapter I (numerous small legs, armored back, jaws), but the precise words for *bug* or *roach* (German: *Insekt* or *Kakerlaker*) are not mentioned. The servant, however, may not be entirely correct in identifying Gregor. The German word *Ungeziefer* in the first sentence, which we have made *pest*, can sometimes be translated as *vermin*, but *vermin* more often means rat or other intrusive animal, rather than a bug.

Raindrops

The minute details in the text of raindrops falling illustrate a central existentialist concept: that which exists in the immediate moment is of paramount importance. The description could also be interpreted as a metaphor for human individuality being destroyed, one person at a time.

Tenants

The three tenants may be an allusion to the Holy Trinity; the German name for them literally translates as "room gentlemen." The German word for *gentleman* (German: *der Herr*) means essentially the same as *lord* and is used both for other humans and God.

Vagueness

There are several places in *The Metamorphosis* where Kafka makes very vague statements, leaving out key clarifying statements or qualifications. For instance, he indicates that Grete cannot stand the smell in Gregor's room. Is it Gregor who smells, or is it the rotten food that she brings him to eat and the trash that seems to accumulate there? There are also odd events thrown in that are never explained, like the butcher's apprentice who carries a basket up the stairwell at the end of the story. In addition, Kafka never even explains how Gregor becomes an insect to begin with. This draws the reader's attention away from the story's plot and causes the reader to focus on the details that Kafka does include.

Vocabulary

abstained – chose to go without

acrid – sharp, unpleasant, or caustic

albeit – even though, although

arbitrary – without basis; subjective

articulation – the effort put forth to pronounce words

asphyxiation – death from lack of air; strangulation

attenuate – to diminish gradually

auspicious – promising; apparently favorable

congealed – thickened or hardened

conservatory – a school that trains students in one of the fine arts

conspicuous – noticeable, obvious

contemplation – thought; consideration

copious – abundant or numerous

credenza – a bookcase, sideboard, or buffet

cut any ice with <someone> [colloquial] – to not make any impression on somebody

differentiate – to distinguish; to see differences

diminutive – very small or tiny

emaciated – thin from lack of nourishment

exuberant – enthusiastic; visibly glad

fervor – great enthusiasm

foresight – the ability to predict or anticipate the future

frugality – miserliness; ability to save money

hitherto – up to this point

immaculate – spotlessly clean or pure

incessant – without stopping; never-ending

indispensable – necessary; unable to live without

indistinguishable – difficult to tell one item from another

inexorable – unable to be stopped

interceding – pleading on someone's behalf

interim – meanwhile; the time between

intermingled – mixed-in or dispersed among

irrepressibly – unable to be hidden or held back

lamentably – unfortunately, sadly, pitifully

meticulously – with great care and attention to detail

minion – a slave; lackey

myriad – numerous beyond counting

perambulatory – of or relating to walking or strolling

perspective – a view or mental outlook

ponderous – very heavy and clumsy

premonition – an inkling; an idea of what will happen

rampant – happening without restraint; widespread

recoup – to make up for; to take in

relentlessly – without pause; without becoming tired or slowing down

relished – savored or enjoyed

resolutely – with determination; forcefully

rue – to regret deeply

scrupulously – conscientiously and exactly; principled

self-reproach – deep regret or self-blame

smorgasbord – a large array and variety (usually of food)

sonorous – deep, resonating, or full of sound

superfluous – more than is needed; unnecessary

taut – tightly stretched

tractable – able to be lead or persuaded

traipse – to walk or plod aimlessly

undulation – wave-like motion

vapid – lacking interest; dull

Insightful and Reader-Friendly, Yet Affordable

Prestwick House Literary Touchstone Classic Editions– The Editions By Which All Others May Be Judged

Every *Prestwick House Literary Touchstone Classic* is enhanced with Reading Pointers for Sharper Insight to improve comprehension and provide insights that will help students recognize key themes, symbols, and plot complexities. In addition, each title includes a Glossary of the more difficult words and concepts.

For the Shakespeare titles, along with the Reading Pointers and Glossary, we include margin notes and various strategies to understanding the language of Shakespeare.

Special Introductory Educator's Discount – At Least 50% Off

New titles are constantly being added; call or visit our website for current listing.

		Retail Price	Intro. Discount
200102	**Red Badge of Courage, The**	$3.99	$1.99
200163	**Romeo and Juliet**	$3.99	$1.99
200074	**Heart of Darkness**	$3.99	$1.99
200079	**Narrative of the Life of Frederick Douglass**	$3.99	$1.99
200125	**Macbeth**	$3.99	$1.99
200053	**Adventures of Huckleberry Finn, The**	$4.99	$2.49
200081	**Midsummer Night's Dream, A**	$3.99	$1.99
200179	**Christmas Carol, A**	$3.99	$1.99
200150	**Call of the Wild, The**	$3.99	$1.99
200190	**Dr. Jekyll and Mr. Hyde**	$3.99	$1.99
200141	**Awakening, The**	$3.99	$1.99
200147	**Importance of Being Earnest, The**	$3.99	$1.99
200166	**Ethan Frome**	$3.99	$1.99
200146	**Julius Caesar**	$3.99	$1.99
200095	**Othello**	$3.99	$1.99
200091	**Hamlet**	$3.99	$1.99
200231	**Taming of the Shrew, The**	$3.99	$1.99
200133	**Metamorphosis, The**	$3.99	$1.99

PRESTWICK HOUSE, INC.
"Everything for the English Classroom!"

Prestwick House, Inc. • P.O. Box 658, Clayton, DE 19938
Phone (800) 932-4593 • Fax (888) 718-9333 • www.prestwickhouse.com

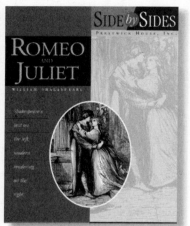